*Summer*

*of*

*Love*

# THE RETURN

Sequel to Auspicious Journey

BRUCE JUNIOR WEST

Summer of Love is dedicated to Connie Ann West - Enduring Muse, Life-long Companion, and Forever Sweetheart, who wrote me a letter every day I was in Viet Nam.

Summer of Love is also dedicated to David Lawrence Black, 1948-2024, a recipient of the Silver Star, the Bronze Star and three Purple Hearts.

He was a decent, kind, wise and fearless advocate for other veterans, as well as an affectionate and loving husband, father and grandfather.

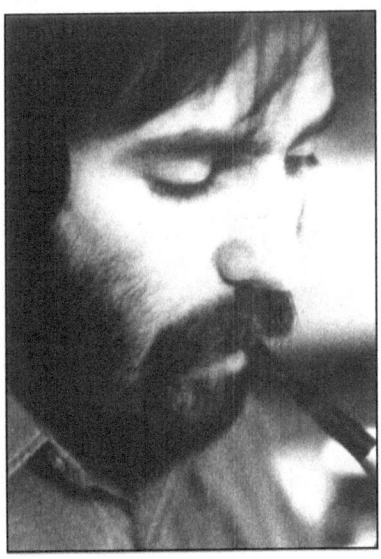

# Chapter One

## Wolf at the Door

Lilly and Dan were married in the Summer of Love. It was 1967, and the world was hurtling toward a thrilling and unknown future. The "pill" had freed women from the crippling fear of an unwanted pregnancy and a new generation of young people were free to express their feelings for one another, as well as the world around them.

Everything changed. The promise of equality seemed within their grasp. The on-ramps in San Luis Obispo and Santa Barbara were packed with long lines of young people "going to San Francisco."

He and Lilly drove through the countryside for hours listening to songs such as "Treat Your Children Well," and "Where Will the Children Play?"

They embraced the generational anthem of Jesse Colin Young and the Youngbloods singing, "Let's Get Together" at Monterey Pop. Young men and women addressed each other as "brothers and sisters." Lilly and Dan walked among the Hippies from the Haight, the long hairs and the short hairs, tie-dyes and school clothes, and no one cared about the differences. It truly was the Summer of Love.

They witnessed their changing world where men and women and the young and old of all races were equal, all valued and treated with respect and love. They accepted the beauty and promise of the life before them. They shared long talks about how they wished to treat each other and how they would care for their children who would someday come to be with them for a while.

But the cruelty of the corrupt war and its corrupt draft dogged their lives. Dan and Lilly clung to their life together carving out each moment, waiting for the next letter, a wolf at the door, tearing them apart, dragging them off to war.

# Chapter Two

*"Abandon hope all ye who enter here."*

"You ain't seen shit."

Dan had torn himself away from Lilly with the torment of their lingering goodbyes and taken the Greyhound to Port Hueneme. Waiting for the next shuttle bus to the base he dropped his sea bag and found a place to sit in the lobby.

An old man sat in the middle of three grimy plastic chairs wedged between the quarter lockers and the free publications. His worn field jacket was covered with combat medals from past and distant wars.

"You ain't seen shit."

Time and wine had left him overcooked and hard-wrinkled. "Got a smoke for an ol' soldier?" It was less a question than a tired chant.

He looked across the room at the soldiers waiting for their bus and raised his ragged voice.

"Anybody got a smoke?"

Squirming under his unforgiving eyes that had seen too much, the soldiers tried to ignore him and turned away, laughing to themselves.

He cursed them for their smug, callow disdain. "I was at Guadalcanal. I…was there…I was. Damn It. Anyone got a smoke for a vet?"

He was yelling now, turning to the room where people were being careful to pretend he did not exist at all. "I was a marine…I was there…you bunch of no good…" His voice trailed off to a whisper… "*bastards.*"

Between his fingers, the old man mumbled, "The war…you don't…how 'bout a smoke?" No one was listening. Dan sat watching the used-up old soldier. He raised his head and looked at Dan, unexpectedly clear-eyed and terribly sane, and said, "I was like you once."

Dan held his gaze, nodded, beginning to understand. The old man repeated, "I was."

The shuttle bus pulled in and stopped just outside the door with the engine idling. Dan stood up, crossed the room, and took the old Marine's hard, blooded hands in his own.

The old vet clutched Dan's hands, looked him in the eye, and said, "I was like you, once."

"I believe you," Dan said, nodding his head. "I believe you."

"Gotta smoke?"

This old soldier reminded Dan of Dante's ferryman at the River Styx, and he wondered if the cigarette somehow served as the coin for his passage.

Still holding the rough old hands Dan wished he had a cigarette to give him. Instead, all he could say was, "I'm sorry, I don't smoke."

The old Marine's grip on Dan's hand softened, as he looked him in the eye and said, "You will."

## Chapter Three

## The Cost of Doing Business

Leaving Okinawa for Viet Nam, the big plane followed the gentle curve of the Ryukyus south and west toward the war, each island becoming smaller until the last tiny speck of land disappeared into the sea.

At that moment it finally became clear to him. He had no way out. Like it or not, he was going to the war - the killing place. What was *he* prepared to do? What would it take to survive this war – this giant tantrum of old men – this deadly drama where nothing was as it seemed?

Lilly! - what price would he have to pay to see her sweet smile, to look upon her beauty, to be in her arms again?

*What price would he pay?*

What would he have to do to see her again?

Dan imagined the dead and dying, the bleeding, the women, and children, and old people, face down with a mouthful of dirt.

*The mysterious enemy*, whoever that might be, who would end his life in this land so far away from home - from her.

Who was this enemy? How would he know them when they came?

Would he tear them apart with his hands? Would he gouge out their eyes? Would he hack them into pieces, pierce their hearts with his knife?

Would he choke them until they could breathe no more?

Would he stomp their brains into the dirt?

Would he break *The Commandment that* says, *"Thou shalt not kill."*

Would he kill?

It was too late to wonder, too late to turn back now. There was no way out.

He would do any, or all the above, and gladly.

*What then of his soul?*

God help him.

## Chapter Four

### Pall Malls

He remembered the old Marine at the bus station in Port Hueneme telling him that he would start smoking when the shooting started. Well, the shooting started soon after he landed in Da Nang. Now, here he was, digging through a carton of 'C' rations for that little red box of Pall Malls.

Dan had to laugh at himself. King-sized, unfiltered Pall Malls - like a small cigar. It wasn't that he had become a smoker. He didn't even like cigarettes. Smoking was just one of the few pleasures available to a person trapped in the middle of a war.

The other pleasure was the mail. The mail where a letter from Lilly was waiting for him every day. He shared the cigarettes, but not the letters. Those, he folded and tucked into his shirt pocket next to his heart.

It was the Tet Offensive of 1969, and Dan was still trying to trade the heavy leather boots he had been issued for a pair of lightweight jungle boots. He had broken into a sweat as soon as he stepped off the plane, and any means of surviving the heat and humidity was welcomed. Dan discarded his under-shirts and shorts and cut off the shirt sleeves and pant legs of his Marine Corps greens. He traded cigarettes for a pair of second-hand jungle boots, figuring they belonged to someone who wouldn't be needing them.

The saluting and the 'yes sirs' and 'no sirs' were exchanged for a .45, an M-16, and live ammunition. No surprise, everything changed. The annoying organizational quirks of the stateside military either disappeared or began to make an odd sort of sense once the battalion unpacked and prepared to defend itself.

Dan was assigned to the Civic Action Program in the neighboring village of Hoa An. He was curious about the Vietnamese. Everything about them was so different than he had ever imagined.

Once the Tet was over, he began leaving the base to explore the local villages. Fascinated, he observed the children on their way to school, and the women on their way to market where they traded everything from a baby pig to a pancake discarded from an American chow hall.

Every sound caught in his ears - the guttural and high-pitched voices of a strange language - *Toi koung noi* - what did it mean? A bicycle bell - the soft beep of a horn, the putt-putt-putter of an overloaded pedicab, the quiet murmur of life on life's terms, all seasoned with the unmistakable pungent scent of nuc-mam made from the vinegar of fermented fish.

One thing he didn't hear was people arguing or yelling at one another. Neither did he hear the sound of a baby crying.

He was amazed at the sight of a schoolgirl in an impossibly clean ao-dai riding a tide of sincere intentions and precious innocence, clutching last night's poem to share with her teacher.

And behind it all, the prelude to the song of war. The rumble of the kettle drums and the thick strings of the double bass - the black smoke and industrial smell of the iron diesels.

## Chapter Five

### Changes

War changes everyone, whoever is touched by it. The soldier, the sailor, the pilot. The cook, the medic, the doctor, and the nurse. The mother and the father, the brother and the sister, and the wife or girlfriend left behind. It has that power over all of us.

Dan knew he was changing day-by-day with each atrocity he witnessed. Each disgraceful theft, unjust murder, and reprehensible rape. He couldn't write to Lilly about it because he didn't want to lose her by becoming someone she didn't know—someone she couldn't love. It hadn't been part of the deal when they had picked out her ring and shared their vows. Now, that person she had married was being pushed and pulled into someone he didn't recognize, so how could she? Indeed, how could he even expect her to?

He wrote her about his experiences at the Bo De School– the children, the teachers, and the old carpenter building the desks of teak for the students.

And he wrote about taking the miracle of medicine to the villagers in the back of his truck. He saw those events as positive and something she could imagine him doing and perhaps even being proud of him for.

But he didn't write about the baked-in racism of the American military which tended to see all Vietnamese as the enemy. Nor did he write about the atrocities, large and small, committed upon the Vietnamese women.

Perhaps because of his love for Lilly, the abuse of the women was the hardest part of the war for Dan to bear. He understood that each of these women was someone's sweetheart, wife, daughter, sister, or mother. He also understood that they embodied the instincts and determination to conceive, carry, birth, nurse and protect their children, so that the dreams of their ancestors could endure for another generation.

And now, witnessing the war crush them until their dreams were extinguished, ground out in the dirt, he realized they were no different than Lilly, who was waiting on the other side of the planet, crossing off the days until his return. What kind of karma were we creating with this war?

What would her fate be when this war finally came to the shores of America?

# Chapter Six

## Coming Home

For now, at least some part of him was going home. Dan looked out the window watching the Bay of Da Nang slip out of sight under the wing of the Boeing 707.

*He remembered taking a previous flight to meet Lilly in Honolulu for a week of rest and recuperation. When Dan had discovered that none of the married men in the battalion had ever been on RnR, and that the Senior Chief was trading their RnRs for sex, drugs, and multiple trips to the whorehouses of Bangkok he realized that he would not see Lilly as promised. And so, he had entered the Senior Chief's office, approached the clerk's desk, and said, "I want my RnR."*

*The clerk had looked up and said, "They've all been given out."*

*Dan asked, "What do you mean, given out."*

*"There's no more. The Senior Chief has used up our allotment."*

*"For his pals, right?"*

*The clerk nodded his head, shrugged, and then looked back down at the papers on his desk.*

*When he glanced up Dan was still there. "I want my RnR."*

*The clerk started to say something when Dan asked, "He has to cross that little footbridge to go to his hootch at night, right?"*

*The clerk nodded. Dan didn't raise his voice or menace the clerk. He just said matter of fact, "Okay, I will be there tonight and I will cut his fucking throat."*

*He wasn't angry. He didn't yell. At the time it just seemed like the next best thing to do.*

*The clerk stared at Dan, who said, "Now, I'm going to go up and sharpen my knife. Thanks for bein' straight."*

*The next thing he knew, he was summoned back to the office and the clerk handed Dan the orders for his RnR.*

*A few days later he was in Honolulu. Lilly had separated herself from the crowd and came striding across the tarmac like a supermodel with a big smile and a kiss. She draped a lei of flowers around his neck and took him in her arms.*

*He didn't know what to do. He had wondered if she would be able to tell what he had become. He felt dirty - ruined - with the stink of the war still on him, in him - a part of him thinking that he did not belong here with her, afraid to touch her, wondering how long before he could be back to the village where he belonged — an imposter in his own country, in his own body.*

***

But now, he was finally going home. This was real. He sat awake and silent, looking out the window, gripping the arms of the seat, repeating under his breath, *Home-Home-get me Home.*

Mt. Shasta came up over the horizon silhouetted in the morning sun. The rest was ocean. The big plane slowly turned and angled down the coast of California.

The word rolled down the aisle. "Port Hueneme is fogged in. We're going on to L.A.

International. You'll be bussed back to Port Hueneme and released from there."

*No! Wrong way!* Another day of airports and buses and waiting. Farther away from home, farther from Lilly, somewhere down below waiting for him. Hours of holding his breath. *Let me go. Let me go Home.*

They flew on. Word came down that the pilot intended to attempt a landing at Pt. Mugu, only a few miles from the Battalion's homeport of Port Hueneme.

Dan stared out the window. Fog. Fog. Fog. The big plane started down. Nobody could see anything. The windows streaked with moisture. Lower and lower. Still nothing but fog. It looked like the plane was going into the water. He begged, *Please don't kill me now.*

Waves, whitecaps broke through the fog. The plane shuddered as the landing gear dropped into place. All at once there was a strip of beach and the concrete landing strip. They were down, every man cheering - a standing ovation.

Out the window, Dan saw a lone family by the side of the airstrip. A junior grade officer with his wife and two young children stood at attention holding a small American flag. The loneliness of the family and the pathos of their gesture seemed to foreshadow what he could expect in this strange land that used to be his home.

Dan dragged his sea bag onto the empty Greyhound bus, stumbled down the aisle and stretched out full-length on the big back seat. Sinking into the comforting rumble of the big diesel engine, he finally slept.

He slept through Ventura, Santa Barbara, Buellton, and Santa Maria. He only opened his eyes from time to time to make sure the waters of the Pacific were still in the west and the mountains of the Sierra Madre were still in the east where they belonged.

Nestled in among the mountains and hills, San Luis Obispo seemed small, strange, and almost quaint. Dan took a cab to the little home Lilly had prepared for them. She met him at the door. He dropped his sea-bag and she took him to bed, holding him while what was left of him, wept in her arms.

# Chapter Seven

## The Letter

It had been over five years since Dan had returned from Viet Nam. He had a decent job and he and Lilly had purchased a home near the coast. Lilly had blessed them with a daughter in kindergarten and a son in nursery school.

He had done his part in the war and believed it was behind him. And then, on a Saturday afternoon, the letter from Ong De arrived in their mailbox. The tattered and worn envelope bore silent testimony to the countless miles, the many years, and the faithful hands that had carried it to him. Dan imagined how his dear friend and teacher Ong De, had approached the gate of an American base, beseeching someone to mail the letter to America, to his friend, Dan, somewhere on the other side of the world.

He sat down on the curb and carefully sliced open the envelope with his pocketknife. Ong De's handwriting, so precise and clear, was so very much like the man himself.

*Dear Sir Daniel,*

*Chaplain Hu and I continue our work with the children and orphans at the Bo De School. However, conditions are not the same as when you were here. Each day now it becomes more and more difficult with more and more orphans and students to care for. I am writing to ask for your help in any way you are able.*

*I recall our conversations on the veranda with great fondness and pray that you and your family are well.*

*Your friend,*

*Ong De*

In his humble way, he was asking Dan for help with the children at the school, never anything for himself, always the children.

He dearly missed Ong De, his teacher and friend, his patient guide to the mysteries of Asia, but he couldn't help him, and he knew it. The war was long over. Even while he was still in Viet Nam, he was aware that American support for the war was evaporating and the American military commitment had begun to be abandoned under the public relations blanket of "Vietnamization."

Holding the tattered letter in his hand, he understood that whatever civilian postal service may have existed in Viet Nam had been interrupted by decades of armed conflict. He had to accept the reality that he had no way of responding to Ong De's request, even if he had the means to help him, which he did not.

Dan understood that his responsibilities were to Lilly, their children, and the community in which he now lived and worked. Against his own longings, he was forced to accept the reality that, even if Ong De were still alive, he lived on another planet that he could not reach.

Dan took the letter into the house and upstairs to his sea chest that held the photos and mementos from his time in Viet Nam. He held the letter between his fingers as his desolate tears of helplessness bled onto the page. When he could bear it no longer, he released the letter and watched it drop into the bottom of the box where he covered it with the photographs, citations and gifts, his memories of the people of Hoa An.

From what Dan could tell the war had ended in the same strange, tragically surrealistic way it had been conceived, justified, and conducted. The more he tried to make sense of it, the more impossible it became for him to sleep through the night. He often found himself in the spare room sitting at his sea chest sifting through photo after photo of the village, the schools, the children and his friends, the letter from Ong De waiting for an answer he could not give.

Dan wondered where Ong De was now. Had he survived the war? The reeducation camps? Dan's heart turned and dropped into his stomach. He wanted to cry but felt too dead inside even to do that. He had done his duty and was proud of his service but with each passing day, each cruel, thoughtless reproach from his own countrymen, the joy, and honor of doing that duty faded further and further from his reach.

The Glory, the flags and the speeches, the close order drill and the chromed rifle salutes, all seemed to be displayed for the next generation of soldiers who would die face down in the dirt crying for their mother.

Dan didn't have any illusions about the false promises of Duty, Honor, Glory. He knew better. But the searing realization that he was now a pariah in the land of his birth came as a cold shock to his soul. There was no Glory. He had done his Duty, and well, but there would be no Honor. While he was proud of his service, its honor had been lost in the false Homeric mythologies of bronze, steel, blood, and brotherhood.

His only remaining duty was to protect Lilly and the children from the horrors of the war as well as the rejection and scorn of the world in which they now lived because of him.

It was late when he finally joined Lilly in their bed. Asleep, she had turned toward his side of the bed with her hand tucked under her face as if she were waiting for his return. Watching the rise and fall of her breathing, Dan was amazed at the perfection of her young womanly form. Childbirth had left her more beautiful than ever.

He inhaled the intoxicating scent of her hair and skin and breath that washed into the smallest places of his heart. He wanted to touch her and bury his face in the warmth of her skin, but he did not.

The nightmares began shortly after he received the letter.

## Chapter Eight

### Square Peg

After Lilly dropped Dan off at the front door of the Probation Department, she smiled and waved goodbye as she started down the hill. He watched her stop at the light, then turn the corner and disappear from his sight.

Before entering the office, he stopped for a moment to look at the building where he was now employed. It had been built in the Spanish style as a hospital to care for patients afflicted with tuberculosis. Solid poured-in-place concrete walls were painted white and capped with a red roof of Spanish tiles. Graceful brick steps led to the entry of sturdy double doors.

It was a serious building with a serious purpose. First designated as a place of care, it was now a significant component of the local system of criminal justice. It was a place where offenders came face-to-face with the laws and expectations of their community and how they had violated its values. It was also a place where they could regain the citizenship they had squandered by the antisocial actions they rarely understood. With standards of supposed objectivity, fairness, and accountability, it was also a place of casual cruelty and at other times, a place of mercy.

Dan's office was in the Juvenile Division that stretched away to his right. The adult offender officers were located in the wing to his left.

He pulled the door open, stepped through the entry and said good morning to the receptionist.

She smiled, "Good morning Dan. Was that the missus dropping you off?"

"Yes, it was. She sees the doctor today."

"How's she coming along?"

"Six months and going strong."

"Is this your second?"

"Yes, it is." He was pleased that she had asked. "Do I have any messages?"

"No, but there's a staff meeting at nine."

Dan came late and found a place to stand in the

back of the crowded staff room. The Chief was complaining about the lack of funding and how he worked so hard and diligently to secure whatever funds he could. He made it sound like the money was coming out of his own pocket and how fortunate everyone was to have a job and how they all should be "especially grateful" to him.

Looking around the room he said, "The negotiations were brutal folks. They bent us over and stuck it to us good, and they didn't even use Vaseline."

Some of the staff shifted uneasily with the crude remarks. But the other men sitting at the table with him nodded and grinned in agreement. Dan watched from the back of the room, disgusted.

Without warning, the Chief focused on a young woman standing in front of Dan. The room went silent and everyone seemed to be aware of what was going on except for Dan. He leaned against the water-cooler and it let out a loud blub-blub-blub! Everyone turned and looked at him as if they were reading his mind.

The Chief glared at him, then her. After a long silence, he stated so everyone could hear.

"Some people around here seem to think they're something special." He paused for effect. "But let me tell you, no one's too good to work midnights at the juvenile hall."

Dan could see her becoming more and more uncomfortable, shifting her weight from one foot to the other and wringing her hands behind her back. He could also see that she was angry and embarrassed, while at the same time trying to keep her head up, and not let anyone see her squirm.

Some of the other men leered at her, seeming to take some twisted pleasure in her humiliation, or perhaps wondering when it would be their turn with her.

"What the hell's going on?" he quietly asked Phil, another new hire, who was standing next to him.

"Don't you know? He's been bangin' her for months - 'til she got sick of it and finally turned him down."

Dan looked at the Chief, shaking his head in disgust.

Phil whispered, "Take it easy man."

None of this was making any sense at all. Dan left the staff room as soon as the meeting was over. He went to the men's room and washed his hands and face. Being in the same room with the Chief reminded him of the Battalion Senior Chief and how it had made him feel dirty to be around him.

Leaving the men's room, he ran into Phil in the hall. "What the hell was that about?"

Phil laughed. "You don't think she'd do that cheesy old bastard if she didn't have to, do ya?"

Dan asked, "Why the hell would she ever want to?"

Phil looked at him like he was a child who didn't understand there was no Santa Claus. "She's got an assignment she loves. She's got a sweet deal and doesn't want to work anywhere else. She either bangs him or she gets transferred to midnights at the Juvenile Hall and her job's filled with someone 'a little more cooperative.'"

Phil started to walk away then turned around and said, "Plus if she ends up working midnights she will have to pay for child care, which she will not be able to afford, so she will have to quit and try to find a job somewhere else or lose custody of her two little girls."

"She's divorced?"

"Yeah, and her old man, who's a buddy of the Chief's, is behind this too. You know, just to fuck with her and get custody of the girls."

Dan walked back to his office shaking his head. He'd expected something different. His community, his home was here. He had been raised here, treated well, given an education, given a chance. But somehow this had all changed. This arrogant assault on everything he believed and everything he had fought for, seemed like a rerun of a bad movie starring the same mindless corruption of the military he had witnessed in Viet Nam.

When he returned to his office there was a large manila envelope on his desk. He wanted to go home but he was curious. It was his probationary evaluation. There was a note to "read and sign."

Dan read the general comments.

"…can be creative…"

Okay.

"...misses staff meetings..."

True.

All things considered, Dan thought it was a pretty accurate evaluation. But then at the last, there was a more general comment noting that he seemed to be "a square peg in a round hole."

He laughed out loud. He wasn't sure how it was meant but he decided to take it as a compliment.

That night after dinner he discussed it with Lilly. "I got my evaluation, Lil."

She raised her eyebrows like she expected great news. He appreciated her faith in him, but he didn't wish to disappoint her, so he tried to make light of it.

He chuckled, "It said I am 'a square peg in a round hole.'"

"What does that mean?"

"I think it means I don't quite fit in."

He didn't want to tell her about the staff meeting that was low and ugly and had no place in their home. But it was eating him up and he had to tell someone.

"It was messed up Lil. The Chief was saying all kinds of weird, inappropriate comments and if that wasn't bad enough, he went after this woman who was standing there in front of me. It was cruel, and sick. I thought I had left that kind of garbage behind in Viet Nam. I really didn't expect it here, not in my town and not in the criminal *justice* system, for Christ's sake."

She asked, "What can you do about it?"

"Don't know."

"Do you want to quit? Go somewhere else?"

"There's nowhere else to go Lil." He turned and looked at her sweet face. "This is our home. To hell with 'em, I'm not going anywhere."

He took her hand and held it saying, "I know this sounds corny, but this is our home. We met here. The people in San Luis were good to me, to both of us. They gave us a chance to get an education. When I drive through town, I feel it. I feel that gratitude every day. I wouldn't do this work anywhere else.

"Besides, I love the work. It suits me. I don't fit into this organization any more than I did in the battalion in Viet Nam, but in the same weird way I seem to be well suited to the work."

She tried not to let him see her disappointment in him, but it was there in her eyes, and he couldn't blame her. He went on, hoping she would understand.

"One thing I learned in Viet Nam is that when the corruption takes over you have a choice. You can go along with it, or you can do something about it. You can try to ignore it but that usually breaks down before long. Some people believe they can 'go along to get along.' Some want to look the other way. Either way, they're part of it and the stink's on 'em for good."

Dan paused, took a deep breath, and said, "That's the way it was overseas. I'd hoped it would be different here but in so many ways it's just the same, or worse. I just don't want any part of it, Lil."

She asked, "How can you work there and not become part of it?"

"I don't know."

"What are you going to do?"

"My job." He paused. "I'm just gonna do my job - my duty."

"And what's that?"

"I'm not sure. Sometimes it feels like I'm back in the same old dirty war."

She didn't say anything, just looked at him from the other side of the table that seemed as far away as the Asian shore where a part of him still stood, looking back.

# Chapter Nine

## The Wall

Duty, Honor, Glory. He had done his duty–
and well–but where was the honor? For sure there
was no glory. In Dan's war, there had been no flag
of battle and no one to pick up the flag if he fell. He
hadn't asked for it, but his duty had been clear. So,
he had returned to the village the next day and the
next and the next.

While it was possible that he could have
been killed in a mortar attack, a rocket, or by a
sapper's bomb, he always figured that it was most
likely that he would be tortured and assassinated.

*Dan stood by the graveyard in Hoa An. The
morning air was still relatively cool, the village was
quiet, and he was supposed to meet one of the
elders.*

*A man Dan recognized as Ong Thai emerged
quietly out of the bamboo. He was alone. Dan
turned to greet him, and they bowed as peers,
crossing their hands at the elbows. Although he was
younger than the other elders, Ong Thai was*

*usually included when important decisions were made. He was always neatly dressed, and Dan never saw him without his white cotton fedora.*

*He signaled for Dan to come with him. "Come school. You see new school."*

*Ong Thai's English wasn't any better than Dan's Vietnamese so, as they had no one to interpret, they took their time walking together, taking care to understand. Listening carefully to one another, their thoughts and feelings focused on their concern for the village and its way of life.*

*The sounds of the village and the immediate cares of the day began to fade into the background. The differences in their two cultures became less and less important as the urgent truth of their hopes and fears merged into a quiet, certain place they shared.*

*Dan respected Ong Thai because he never failed to act with sincere concern and care for the village and the people in it. He was always serious. Dan had never seen him laugh or even smile. It seemed as if Ong Thai could see the vast horror of the war hanging over the village like a giant hammer poised to smash his home, his family, his way of life, everything he had ever loved.*

*The trail through the bamboo opened into a clearing. Ong Thai stopped and gestured with his open hand. "Nha troung," (schoolhouse) "We make."*

*It was a small, one-room schoolhouse, lovingly made from lumber Dan had salvaged and hauled to the village in his truck. The villagers had very carefully fit the different pieces of the plywood puzzle together to make a school they were proud of.*

*Stepping inside, Ong Thai used his pocketknife to probe the joints and show Dan how carefully they had been fit together. "See, no sun, no sun."*

*Dan stood amazed at the work and dedication evident in the humble little schoolhouse. Beaming with pride, Ong Thai held Dan's hand as they walked back out into the sunshine and stood looking at the new school.*

*Dan was aware that this part of the village was closest to the road and was bordered on the south by an area that was controlled by deserters, warlords, and criminal gangs. He sensed that this little school symbolized these people's unwavering commitment to a decent life in the face of the worst kinds of chaos just outside their door.*

*Ong Thai gestured with his palm down for Dan to follow, leading him on down the trail toward the southern border of the village.*

*The bamboo gradually fell away, opening to a large, irregular meadow where the trail curved around a low, grass-covered mound. The trail dropped away on the other side to reveal the twisted, ruined body of a young American soldier. He was laying awkwardly, face down, his hands tied behind his back. A gunnysack was tied over his head, covering his face that was turned away and down into the grass as if he were sleeping.*

*Dan looked around the edges of the meadow, the bamboo. Who had done this? Who were they? Where were they? Were they watching him now?*

*His vision narrowed until all he could see was the body in front of him. There was no sound. He felt drunk, the kind of drunk he wouldn't remember. He tried to walk but couldn't feel his feet. The ground felt hard and slippery. He was cold inside, not angry, not afraid, but stunned, curious, frozen in place.*

*Who? Why? What could this person have possibly done to deserve such a death?*

*He took a deep breath and stumbled across the mound and knelt beside the body where the blood and bodily fluids had soaked into the earth. It hadn't yet started to smell of rot, but it wouldn't be long. Using the sharp tip of his knife Dan pulled the blood-soaked shreds of the gunnysack away from the boy's face. The eyes and eyelids, ears, lips and nose, the tender parts, were gone, leaving only the teeth marks of the rats. Ong Thai came to his side and speaking in quiet, precise Vietnamese told him what the villagers had seen from the bamboo. Dan didn't understand the words, but somehow he understood what the man was saying.*

*The gunnysack had been stuffed with a couple of the big, hungry rats that had grown fat and aggressive on the greasy by-products of the war. Then the bag of rats had been tied over the man's head.*

*Against his will, Dan couldn't help but imagine the rats biting, clawing, chewing while the soldier ran, frantically shaking the bag on his head, trying to throw them off, the frenzied rats feeding on his eyes and then on through the eye sockets and along the optic nerves into the tender, sweet tissue of the brain.*

*There was a small clump of bamboo on the mound that had been cut at an angle, leaving sharp ends sticking out of the ground, and at some point the man had impaled himself on the sharp ends of the cut bamboo, driving it through the gunny-sack, through his eye socket and into his brain. It was hard to tell if he was trying to kill himself or the rats that were eating him alive, or maybe both.*

*After gorging on the sweet meat of the brain, the rats had gnawed their way out of the gunnysack and waddled away through the grass.*

*Standing up, Dan swallowed his disgust and his fear. He took a deep breath and looked around the clearing, the sweet M16 a certain comfort in his hand. He and Ong Thai stood over the body, looking at each other for a long time, trying to understand.*

*In his mind, he could see the beast, the dogs of war with its army of rats in a dark cloud of blood lust over the land. Bloated and arrogant, it waited patiently with a bloody grin, knowing it had already won.*

*Dan stepped back and shook his head. "Who did this?" He asked, pointing to the head, the body, the bloody gunnysack. He was somehow detached. It was all like a movie, a horrible black and white "second feature" that he would have to get out of his head before he could ever go to sleep again.*

*Ong Thai looked at him until their breathing slowed in unison. He lifted his gaze away from Dan to the edge of the meadow then slowly around to each clump of bamboo, each mound of grass, each dark shadowed recess where someone could be watching.*

*"People watch...people say...numba ten GI."*

*"Deserters?"*

*Ong Thai nodded, "Numba Ten GI."*

*Ong Thai looked north, toward where the trail came into the clearing from Hoa An.*

*"People watch, people see."*

*Ong Thai turned toward him, eye to eye. "You too much alone Dan-i-el. Bad people, bad people do this."*

*Dan took Ong Thai's hand and held it, bowing his head, wondering, how could anyone do such a horrible thing? How could they even imagine it?*

*He shuddered as death's black hand brushed the back of his neck.*

Forcing himself across that uncertain boundary, through that thin membrane, into the village, swallowing his fear, pushing it down, pounding it deep into his guts and holding it there. The price of admission each day.

Now, when every other duty, every shred of honor had been stripped away, the one duty that remained clear to him was to protect his family from the war. He had told them about the Bo De School, the children, and his friends in the village, but not the atrocities, small and large, and the deprivations of humanity at its worst, or the sounds and smells of innocent people burning alive.

He didn't have an anniversary date like most veterans. But his war, Dan's war, had stamped his soul every day he had swallowed another bag of rats and entered the village by himself. Now that he was home, he began to realize that he had carried that same bag of rats, the very thing he despised the most, home in his guts.

The nightmares had begun not long after the letter's arrival. Ong De came to him in a dream, his face appearing from the dark shore, his black eyes asking, "Where are you, my friend? Why did you leave?

It wasn't long before the sound of the mason's trowel entered Dan's dreams, buttering each brick, *schhnick, schhnick*, building his own prison, brick by brick, no windows, no doors. With no way out, he raised the walls around himself vainly trying to protect the people he loved from what he had become.

Now, the night dreams came in the faces of the other people he had left behind, the dear friends he had abandoned to the war.

Ong De, his teacher and friend, Ong Wat, the old farmer who had been like his own father and friend, Ba Wi, his Vietnamese mother and Ong Trong, the old Confucian. One by one they came to him in his dreams, their faces rising out of the dark pit of the war.

As he built his own prison the night dreams turned into the bag of rats coming for him out of the dark. The darkness became the black bag stretching up and over his head and the faces of his friends were replaced by the rats crawling over the lip of the bag, teeth gnawing, reaching for his eyes. Rats, big, black, and hungry, their bloody fangs, foul with the stench of death, clashing like steel on the blade of a sword. They flew at his face, his ears, lips, nose, and eyes. Always the eyes–the stinking whiskers scratching across his face.

The bag closed over his head and he woke up arms flailing, naked in the middle of their bedroom, fighting, trying to tear off the bag, striking out with his hands, tearing the rats off his face, and flinging them across the room. Lilly, awake on the bed, looked at him as if he had become some maniacal stranger who had forced his way into their life. He knew she was concerned for him but at the same time, he couldn't stand to see the confusion and fear in her eyes now, when she looked at him. It seemed as if she were wondering, *What would he do next?*

He began sleeping alone, staying up late to avoid the dream cycle, then hauling himself out of bed in the morning to the alarm clock. He avoided groups of any kind. One night at the Farmer's Market in San Luis Obispo he left Lilly looking at the tomatoes and fled from the noise of the crowd, only becoming aware of where he was when he was two blocks away in the back of the credit union parking lot.

When he went back Lilly was still there waiting. She didn't ask him why he had taken off or where he had been. But it left him doubting himself, wondering why he had left her standing in the street and what he would do next. What would he do that he didn't remember? What if he had returned and she wasn't there?

Dan knew something was wrong but didn't know what to do about it. He tried talking to counselors, but the understanding and treatment of trauma still seemed to be carefully hidden, or disguised, behind the classic veils of anxiety and depression too often treated with medications with confusing and harmful reactions disguised as "side effects." Nobody wanted to talk about it. It was taboo.

He had survived the war but not the field of dishonor. Built on a lie it had been a war in name only. Now, looking back, it seemed as if it had been our own Civil War, a manifestation of the massive national guilt - the grim fact of our own history of slavery – a brutal, explosive discharge of our own existential rage visited upon the women and children and old people of Viet Nam, condemned for the color of their skin.

The shame of the war's mindless brutality had followed him home and slept between him and Lilly every night. So, he had left the bed where she had welcomed him home and held him when he had wept. When he could stand it no more, he got up and took his sleeping bag to the sand dunes where the mother's soft voice of the sea washed over him until he slept.

It had seemed the only possible honor left was to protect her and the children from the rotten stench of the war and he swore, and swore, and he swore that he would protect them, hoping somehow in that way that he might grasp and hang on to that last thread of honor left to him from a war that had none.

But it hadn't worked out that way. He had closed himself off from Lilly and the children and held it all inside of himself where it rotted slowly from the inside out. Seeking to protect them, he built the walls higher and double-barred the door to keep them out. And the light of her smile–the light of their love for each other–couldn't break through, and slowly faded and faded, until, like a candle burning down at the wick, flickering, sputtering, in the hot wax. And she tried to reach him in every way she knew, and he tried to reach her in every way he knew, but the dishonor of the war's wasted lives and the stench of its needless deaths laid in the bed between them like Odin's bloody sword.

# Chapter Ten

## Rape Case

Dan stopped at the front desk and checked in with the receptionist. He had three messages, one from an attorney, one from a juvenile's mother and one from a defendant by the name of Paul Pendergast. Mr. Pendergast wished to make an appointment as soon as possible.

Dan walked to his office but before he could sit down Donaldson, his supervisor, stuck his head in the door and said, "Adult Intake is swamped, Dan. Can you help out? We'll start you out with some easy cases."

As he was already assigned to the intensive supervision of juveniles, Dan wondered when he would find the time.

Donaldson said, "Don't worry, you'll get the hang of it."

"When does this start?"

"The files are in your drawer."

Curious, Dan walked down the hall to where his drawer was so stuffed with cases it couldn't be closed. He took the stack from the drawer, lugged them back to his office and dropped them on his desk. Taking a file from the top he sat down and began reading the police report. The defendant was a Paul Pendergast, and it was a felony rape that had been reduced to a misdemeanor.

His thoughts went back to that day in Hoa An when a deserter had wandered into the village holding a grenade. He told one of the boys that he had pulled the pin and "wanted a woman."

Dan remembered watching the .223 round disappear into the dark chamber of his M-16. With that one simple action, he had found himself in the middle of this "war" where right and wrong were never clear. He realized that he could have easily found himself on the "wrong side" of this strange business and never make it back home.

He thought about another time he had watched one of his fellow Americans drag a Vietnamese girl down the hill to the Senior Chief's office. There, a group of men waited to gang rape and beat her almost to death. He still carried the helplessness, frustration, and disgust he had felt at the time. He was helpless then. He wasn't helpless now. Now he represented the law of the land.

He hadn't yet read the police report, but this already made his skin crawl. Now, the black words on the white page, statement of fact, took him back to the frustration and disgust that was still very much a part of him.

From the report, he gathered that Perry, the bar manager, had asked the victim to stay for an "after-hours party." He also surmised that she couldn't see Perry's criminal record or the prison tattoos beneath his expensive new dress shirt.

According to the police report she'd had a few more drinks at the bar then excused herself and started down the hall to the toilet. Meeting her in the hallway, Perry had blocked her way and hit her so hard that she was still unconscious the next morning. A senior citizen walking his dog found her dumped in a parked car. She had been beaten and raped. Her dress was torn and her underwear was missing.

The sexual assault exam confirmed the rape. She identified Perry as the man who had knocked her out. Like she said, "The last thing I remember was him on top of me."

Perry was arrested by the Pismo Beach Police and booked into the County Jail. But then the case took a strange direction. Dan turned the case file over and looked at it again. Perry's name wasn't on it. It was some other guy, a Paul Pendergast, and although it was clearly a serious felony, it had been *reduced to a misdemeanor*. Dan couldn't put his finger on it, but something was clearly wrong with this case.

He opened it and went through it carefully. It was not like clerical to make a mistake but maybe the two cases had somehow been mixed together. He checked the court order. No, that was the way it came in, Pendergast - misdemeanor. What happened to Perry?

Dan called the jail and talked to the booking clerk. "Who bailed out this guy Perry?"

"An attorney flew in from Fresno in his private plane - paid the bail in full."

"In full? Nobody does that."

"The whole thing, cash."

When Paul Pendergast arrived for the interview, he was just like he had sounded on the phone - small and scared with clothes that didn't quite fit. Dan wanted to hear what he had to say.

"I was in the bar."

"After hours?"

"Uh-huh. But I didn't rape the girl."

"Who did?"

"Well, I saw her get up to go to the toilet."

Dan nodded.

"Then that Perry guy jumped up quick and went around the other way and that's the last I saw."

"What did you do?"

"I went home and went to bed."

"So how come your name is on this court order saying you entered a plea on this?"

Paul choked and swallowed hard. "They came and got me the next day. They made me do it."

"Who came and got you?"

He stammered, "That guy Perry, the guy who runs the bar, and this lawyer from Fresno. They came to my house and got me out of bed. I had a hangover. They said they were going to take me down to the police station and I was gonna sign a confession that I did the rape thing."

"And you did it?"

"I did, I mean I signed it. I didn't rape nobody."

"So, why'd you sign it? That makes no sense."

"They said they'd kill my mother."

Dan said, "I'm not buying it."

Pendergast panicked. "They did! They drove me past my mom's house. They knew where she lived! I could see her through the window. She was washing the dishes!"

"So, you went to Pismo Beach PD, made a statement that you raped this woman, and you were allowed to plead to a misdemeanor?"

"Yeah." Paul hunched over, squirming in his chair. "Look, you're supposed to recommend the minimum. That's part of the deal. Don't you wanna know about my past or nothin'?"

"Not really."

"Whatcha gonna recommend?"

"The absolute maximum the law will allow."

"That's not the deal!" Pendergast squealed.

Dan shrugged, "I don't care. You want to be a party to this, that's up to you, but I don't. It stinks and you know it."

"What should I tell 'em?"

"Whatever you want."

None of this made any sense. He felt sorry for Pendergast, but he couldn't help him without becoming part of this crooked deal. Dan watched Pendergast walk down the hill then went looking for someone who knew more than he did. Helen had been a Probation Officer for years and knew everything that went on, or pretty close to it. Better yet, she always told it like it was.

She never missed a day's work. She opened the door every morning at exactly eight o'clock and left exactly at five. She kept to herself, working quietly behind her office door, cases sorted into neat piles on her desk. She dressed modestly in her own quiet style and never raised her voice or offered an opinion unless she was asked. Whenever Dan had asked her advice, she had offered it freely and honestly. More importantly, it had always been helpful.

He knocked on her door. "Helen?"

"Come on in."

"Do you have a minute?"

"I'm ready for a break." She reached for her coffee cup.

"What's up?"

He told her about the rape case. "It just doesn't make sense."

She smiled. "If you expect things around here to make sense, you're going to be sadly disappointed."

Dan shook his head. "I don't get it."

"First of all, Danny boy, you be careful what you're sticking your nose into."

He looked at her, questioning.

She continued, "Look, you're not stupid. PG&E is spending thirteen billion dollars just for the construction out there at Diablo Canyon. That's a lot of money anywhere. When they started spreading that kind of money around in this little cow county, the bad guys landed here with both feet."

"Organized crime?"

"What do you think? They go where the money flows. They bought your little restaurant/bar down there in Shell Beach along with a lot of other joints. They're working 'em as fronts for drugs and girls and whatever else they can turn to their advantage. Your girl, the victim in this case, never should have been in there. She's lucky she wasn't killed and dumped in the ocean. Perry's about as bad as they come. He went to prison for attempted murder and high-jacking trucks. He wasn't any good before he went in and I'm pretty sure he didn't come out any better. The last I heard he was with the Aryan Brotherhood. It looks like right now they're the muscle for the Fresno suits."

"Fresno?"

"Yeah. They've had their hand in here for a long time, pushing drugs and prostitution for the soldiers at Camp Roberts and Fort Hunter Liggett."

Dan didn't say anything. Helen looked at him across her desk and asked, "You say they paid his bail in full?"

"Yeah."

"That should tell you something. When's the last time that happened?"

She turned back to the cases on her desk, and he understood his time was up.

"Thanks, Helen."

"You're welcome. Like I said, watch your step. They're used to getting their way. They think that's the way it's supposed to be and they really don't like it when someone gets in the way."

...

Will Lawson was over four hundred pounds and chain-smoked Kent cigarettes. The huge ashtray on his desk looked like an aircraft carrier that had been carpet bombed with cigarette butts.

He was from a small town in Texas where he had grown up above the local jail operated by his mother and father. Born into the law, he possessed few illusions about what it was and wasn't.

Notwithstanding his weight, his crew cut, and his rumpled gray suit, he was widely respected to the point that no one called him by his first name. Dan was aware that there was an unusually good mind behind that slow Texas drawl.

He found Mr. Lawson at his desk and waited patiently until he looked up.

"Dan—iel?" He said as slow as humanly possible.

"Can I talk to you about a case?"

"Uh huh."

Dan told him about the rape.

"Misdemeanor you say?"

Dan nodded. He wanted to say it made no sense, but he didn't.

Lawson looked at him, sighed, and reached for his pack of Kents. He lit the cigarette but didn't really draw on it. He just held it close and breathed in and out as the cloud of smoke circled his head.

"Have a seat." He took a thick stack of case files off a chair and dropped them unceremoniously on the floor. "You got an ugly one, don't ya?"

"Seems like it. What I don't understand is why the police and the D.A. went along with it. They gotta know better."

"Let me tell you what you're up against here."

Dan sat down trying to avoid the cloud of smoke.

Lawson stubbed out his cigarette and said, "The last District Attorney to be 'elected' by the people of this county was a fella by the name of James Powell. He was killed while he and his family were on vacation down in Mexico somewhere. That was some time back."

Dan remembered reading about it in the Telegram-Tribune. There was some speculation that it had been a murder but nothing more was ever said.

Dan looked up and said, "I was in high school when that happened."

Lawson looked at him over his glasses. "You remember?"

"I do."

"Okay, whoever's the D.A., steps down in mid-term, and the next guy, whoever they want, is shoehorned in. No attorney in his right mind is gonna run against an incumbent D.A."

He looked at Dan like he was supposed to understand, shook his head, and said, "You could say the 'fix' was in."

Dan was thinking out loud. "So even though the D.A.'s supposed to be an elected position, it's been taken out of the peoples' hands and the D.A. just gets 'appointed' by someone, somewhere?"

"Uh huh, so you can see things are not ex-at-a-ly what they oughta be."

"What about the sheriff?"

"Same story, different buncha characters."

Dan had more questions, but Lawson was done talking.

"Thanks."

"All this ain't what you thought it was gonna be, is it?"

"No, it sure isn't. I guess I expected something different from the law."

Lawson grunted. "Well, Dan—iel, people are people. Sometimes they just ain't so purdy."

He dismissed Dan with a nod, turned back to his desk, and lit another Kent.

Dan called a friend at the D.A.'s office. "What's up with this Pendergast case, Reynolds?"

Silence. After a pause, Reynolds said, "So you got that piece of shit, huh?"

"Uh-huh, I did."

"Who's the Deputy D.A.?"

"Boyle."

"Perfect, Dan, perfect. Boyle's buddy-buddy with your guy Perry."

*"What?"*

"Yeah, he's been hanging out at Perry's place in Shell Beach, or the one in Avila. He's always there. He claims he's doing an 'investigation,' but I think it's more about the girls Perry keeps feeding him."

Dan's skin crawled and he wanted a shower. Reynolds continued, "Look, Dan, it's standard for these guys. Perry knows how to make Boyle feel important."

"Yeah, but that doesn't mean we have to go along with it. What about the girl dumped in the parking lot?"

"She's lucky she's not dead."

"So, when this is over Perry can rape her and beat her up and put her on the streets when he's done with her?"

"It's happened before, Dan."

"What the hell's going on here, Reynolds?"

"You tell me. Whatever it is, it stinks doesn't it."

"Sure does."

"What are you going to recommend?"

"The max. What else can I do? Did you see the police report?"

"I did. But they'll shit if you recommend the max and it'll come right back onto you."

Dan squinted at the phone. "I don't think I have a choice."

"Good luck."

Dan submitted his report and then called Lilly.

She was happy to hear from him. "Hi, honey!"

He took a deep breath. "Ahhh."

She knew something was wrong. "You okay?"

"Yeah. Got a bad case here hon'."

Silence. He could feel her mood slipping away. "I gotta ask you to keep the doors locked and the children in the backyard."

"I got the Blue Birds this afternoon. What am I supposed to do?"

"I don't know. I'll come home."

"The girls would like that."

He laughed. "I can work upstairs."

"I'll save you some cookies."

The court date came and Pendergast called him the same day. "They said to call you right away. Can I come up and talk to you?"

"Sure, come on up."

Pendergast was there in a few minutes, sweating, wringing his hands, and talking fast. "Thanks for letting me come up. I appreciate it. I hope we can work this thing out."

"Has anything changed?"

Pendergast squirmed in the chair. "Like I said before, you're not supposed to recommend the max. They told me you'd go easy on this."

"Who told you that?"

"My attorney, he's got it worked out with the D.A."

"Who's paying for your attorney, Paul?"

Paul looked at the floor and shrugged, "You know."

"And who is the D.A.?"

"Some guy named Doyle."

"You mean Boyle?"

"Somethun' like that. You're supposed to call him, the D.A., and he'll explain it all to you. He said to tell you to call him."

Dan shook his head and said, "Look, Paul, I appreciate your position. The way I see it, you're the perfect patsy. What the heck were you doing in that bar after hours?"

Pendergast shrugged. "Hanging around. Perry was cool to me most of the time."

"You might want to think about why you're taking the rap for people like that. Why are you letting them use you this way?"

Pendergast looked at the floor, shook his head and asked, "What are you going to recommend?"

"Okay, first, this thing got pled to a misdemeanor when you and I both know it's a felony and whoever did it should be in prison."

Dan stopped and took a breath. "Now you tell me that you only entered the plea because Perry and his attorney told you they would kill your mother."

"They will! I know they will!"

"I understand. That's a decision you have to make."

"They're not kiddin' around!"

"I'm not kidding around either, Paul. I have to make a recommendation to the judge for sentencing on this."

"Yeah?" His voice was still hopeful.

"If I go easy like I'm supposed to, then I'm a part of this rape, just like Perry, and just like Boyle and just like you. My name will be on it, just like yours."

"So, you're not gonna help me?"

"You're going to have to help yourself, Paul."

"How?"

"Stand up and tell the truth."

"They'll kill me! They'll kill my poor mother!"

"Maybe they will, maybe they won't, but you have a little time right now to figure out how to protect yourself and your mother. For starters, you could get yourself a decent attorney."

"I don't have that kind of money!"

"Hell Paul, any Public Defender would be better than that shill from Fresno they stuck you with. He's working for the Fresno mob, not you. You know that, don't you?"

Pendergast shrugged, head down.

"If you let them use you for a patsy this time, there will be another and another, and you're going to spend your whole life doing someone else's time."

Paul twisted in his seat and looked across the desk at him.

"You're not helping me!"

"I know, and I'm not going to. What about the girl who was knocked out, raped, and dumped in the back of the car, Paul? Who the hell's helping her?"

The next afternoon Dan called the victim and asked if he could come over and talk to her.

She said, "I was wondering when someone would ask me about this."

He took Phil, another probation officer, with him to where she lived in an older rental on the south side of town. He stood on the porch and gently knocked on the door.

An attractive young woman with short red hair came to the door. She was clutching her robe around her while she looked up and down the empty street. She was scared. Dan could see her boyfriend, hovering in the background, looking over her shoulder at him and Phil.

Dan introduced himself through the screen door. "I'm investigating this case in order to make a sentencing recommendation to the court."

She nodded. Dan said, "I feel like I need to talk to you."

"Thank you," she said sincerely. "Nobody has talked to me since the day that Perry guy and his attorney showed up here."

"They came here?" Dan was incredulous.

"Right there, where you're standing."

"Did they threaten you?"

"What do you think?"

"I don't know."

"They threatened to kill me if I didn't take back my statement to the police."

"Did you?"

"A Pismo Beach police officer showed up right after they left. It was like he was waiting down the street. But like I told them the first time, all I remember is seeing Perry in the hall. He hit me so hard it knocked me out. When I woke up it was pretty clear I had been raped. The exam confirmed it. There was nothing to change."

Dan was sick in his gut with disgust and anger. He looked at the worn floorboards on the porch until he trusted himself to speak. He finally looked up and pointed at her boyfriend hovering uselessly in the background.

"Look, this lady is the only one in this case so far with any guts at all. Why don't you try taking care of her?"

Phil stumbled off the porch behind him. "Man, did you see those tits? Do you think she had anything on under that robe?"

"You're sick, Phil."

"I know!" Phil said grinning.

"Phil! Intimidating a witness, especially a victim, is a fucking felony in the State of California and you are a witness to her statement so quit talking about her god damned tits!"

Phil looked at Dan like he was ruining the fun.

When he got back to the office Dan called Deputy District Attorney Boyle. "I want to report a felony."

"What's that?"

"Your pal, Perry, and his Fresno attorney went to the victim's house and threatened her to change her statement."

Silence.

"What the hell's going on Boyle? The last time I looked, that's still a felony in this state."

Boyle took a deep breath on the other end. "Look, Dan, you just don't understand."

"Understand what?"

"The big picture, the larger law enforcement picture here."

"Indeed."

"You need to go along with this." Boyle was almost whining.

"I'm not changing the recommendation, Boyle."

"That could be a problem."

Dan waited for it to sink in. "Not for me."

Boyle hung up and it didn't take long before Donaldson came looking for him.

"You're late on the Pendergast case again. Do you have the report done?"

"It's been continued."

"Again? How far along are you?"

Dan filled him in.

Donaldson whined, "The Chief got a call from the D.A. He's not too happy with your recommendation."

Dan said, "I'm not surprised."

"Look, Dan, I'm not going to tell you what to write, or recommend, but you need to think of your future here."

He looked at Donaldson and shook his head in disgust. His future? How about the present? How about this stinker of a case that everyone wanted to roll over on? How about the girl dumped in the parking lot?

Dan wanted to call Donaldson a slimy son of a bitch, but he didn't think it would go over too well. Regardless, he wasn't going to change his recommendations.

He said, "Okay. But tell me why they won't file a felony for intimidating a witness?"

"You reported it?"

"To Deputy D.A. Boyle, himself."

Donaldson looked around the room like someone might be listening.

"Forget it Dan. We'll take care of it. Do you have the file?"

Dan pointed to the file on his desk. Donaldson grabbed it and left in a hurry.

Filled with disgust, Dan went to the men's room and washed his hands and face. Then he looked in the mirror and shrugged.

It felt like Viet Nam all over again. He remembered the day he had met with the village elders and they had told him that the Viet Cong's weapon cache had been uncovered and surrendered to the provincial authorities. They had told him how they wished to meet with his commanding officer. He thought about how he had been so thrilled to have *won the peace* in this small corner of the war - and then it had all been thrown away when his commanding officer had said, "I ain't gonna talk to no gook."

But this was different. Here he was not alone. Dan had done his part. He knew that Boyle had been exposed in the report and that he was on his way out as a Deputy District Attorney. Even though the case had been taken away from him, he believed the Judge was aware of the stakes and had his reasons for sending the case back, and back again. Dan was also aware that whoever had doctored the report had put their name on it, and that was something *they* had to live with.

The front page of the Telegram-Tribune was on the table in the staff room. *"County Supervisors hire Sheriff with Cirrhosis of the Liver due to Alcoholism."*

The article went on to report that the new Sheriff had been a high-ranking administrator in the Kern County Sheriff's office. He had been "hired" by the San Luis County Board of Supervisors when the previous Sheriff had stepped down mid-term.

Will Lawson quietly entered the staffroom and dropped all his four hundred pounds into "his chair." Lawson pulled the paper over in front of him, adjusted his glasses and read the headline about the Sheriff.

When he was done, he slid the paper back across the table. "There's our new Sheriff, Dan. Hand-picked by PG&E."

Dan looked at him. "What do you mean?"

"Seabrook nuclear power plant. You musta been overseas. The sheriff back there wouldn't arrest the protesters, claimed they had the constitutional right to peaceful assembly. It caused the utility, don't remember, East Coast somethin' or other, all kinds of grief. PG&E ain't gonna let that happen at Diablo. They got too much on the line."

He stubbed out his cigarette and went on in his Texas drawl. "They've handpicked the Board of

Supervisors, and they've *hired* a drunk for a sheriff. The D.A. wasn't elected, but appointed at mid-term by who knows whom."

Lawson picked up the paper, raised his shaggy eyebrows and said, "Not only that, but I understand that our illustrious County Administrator has been indicted for over a hundred felonies along with the Chairman of the Civil Service Commission, his partner in crime."

Dan was speechless.

Lawson looked at him over the top of his glasses and said, "See what you're up against?"

Dan shook his head. Lawson reached for another Kent and said, "Hang on Danny boy, it's gonna be a sleigh ride."

# Chapter Eleven

## Black Bag

He compartmentalized his days and his nights and that seemed to work for a while. Then the rats followed him into the light of day.

Dan was at his desk when everything changed around him. All he could see was the bag of rats with only a sliver of light around the edges. Distorted images of Lilly and the children reached out to him. Everything else was black. The black sack of rats grew larger and larger, looming above him, reaching up over his head.

It was the same nightmare but now he was awake. The bag closed over his head. The rats came for his eyes.

He stood up and ran but didn't know it. He shoved open the back door and stumbled out into the parking lot. His only instinct was to reach his car and drive away as fast as he could.

Someone grabbed his arm and held on. He tried to pull away but the grip tightened.

"Dan, Dan, what's wrong?" A woman shouted, "What's wrong?"

He shook his head.

She asked again, "What's wrong?"

He cried out, "The rats!"

"The rats?"

He slumped forward in defeat. "The bag of rats. It came for me here."

Her fingers dug into his arm. She wasn't letting go. He heard her voice and tried to look at her. It sounded like his friend Marcie. He could almost see her face. She was telling him something. "You have to love it, Dan! Send it love!"

He lurched back, trying to get away from her, desperate to escape the very thought of it–to reach his car and drive away.

"Love?"

Her grip tightened. "Send it love! Listen to me! When you send it hate and fear it only gets stronger and stronger until it consumes you."

He gagged and was sick in his stomach. "I can't! I can't! I hate it!"

The bag grew closer and larger, looming over his head, teeth gnashing, the rat's whiskers quivering with blood lust.

She shouted, "You have to love it, Dan!"

He groaned, "I can't. It's impossible."

The thought of it made him sick. Love? That was absurd - yet he knew she was right. The rats in the black bag waited, teeth gnashing, waiting for her to let go of his arm. Love? Send it Love?

The bag grew larger, stronger, blacker, coming for him.

She cried, "Send it love!"

He believed her but couldn't force himself to say the words.

Marcie shook his arm and begged him. "Send it love!"

He believed her. He couldn't wait any longer.

He croaked, "Love! I send you love!"

It stopped, retreated just a bit, teeth gnashing. Now, with a whiff of courage, he tried it again. "I send you love!"

The bag shrank, the darkness faded. He could see Lilly and the children around the bright edges of the bag as if they were in the sunshine.

His mind shouted. "Do it! Do it for them!"

He reeled back, caught his balance, and shouted in a shuddering whisper at the bag of rats. "Love! I send you Love!"

His stomach turned into a hard, bitter ball but the bag shrank back slowly losing its power over him.

It worked! He pulled himself erect and in a great silent cry sent it love, again and again until it faded - until it was gone. Marcie let go of his arm and looked him in the face. "You okay?"

The bag was gone, he could see. He nodded and followed her across the parking lot to the back door, back to work, back to his duty - his safe place, one more time.

Dan survived that day and the next. Marcie had pulled him back from the edge and taught him how to survive. The rats were still there in his guts. But just as in Hoa An, and just as his grandfathers and his father had done before him, he would do his duty each day.

## Chapter Twelve

*What Did You Do in the War?*

With each step soft on the forest floor, the trail opened before him, rising through the timber then on up into the naked rocks and peaks of the high country. Dan was on a backpacking trip into the Western Sierra with three other guys, acquaintances from work. They started late and the others had forged on ahead. It was darkening now, but Dan was in no hurry.

The trail came out of the forest on a rocky point where the last bit of sunlight was just fading from the western sky. The others had stopped. One of the guys pointed to a rock fire ring and said, "This looks like a good spot."

Dan dropped his pack and leaned it against a down log. "I'll get some wood."

The darkness closed in around them. The world was reduced to a small circle of light from the fire. Scott had been hired shortly after Dan, and the other two, several years later. They ate and talked about the job.

"Works great," said Dan. "I have no problem with the cases, or the people, but the department is sure different than I ever expected."

"Yeah, me too," said one of the new guys.

Scott said, "We call it 'Casa del Wacko.'"

They laughed and then after a while sat together, looking into the fire. Dan went to pick up some more wood. Returning with his arms full of firewood he stopped to watch the light from the fire dancing through the trees. Someone said "Viet Nam" like it was a dirty word.

Dan stood in the dark waiting for something to change - waiting for a place around the fire where he would feel welcome.

"It was fucked up from the get-go." One of the new guys said, "I'm sure glad I didn't have to go."

"Yeah," the other agreed. "Me too."

"How'd you swing it?" Scott asked.

"I had a medical excuse. My dad knew the doctor."

"And it worked?"

"Yeah, worked great."

The first new guy was flossing his teeth. He extracted the floss from between his teeth, examined it carefully, and volunteered, "I got married and had a kid." He laughed. "I'm not sure which one was worse."

Still holding the floss, he looked up as Dan stepped out of the darkness. "What about you Dan? You weren't stupid enough to go to Viet Nam, were you?"

Dan carefully sat the firewood down and stared at him across the fire. His guts were cold and tight. He turned away from the fire and picked up his pack trying to find the strap in the dark.

Scott noticed his discomfort and tried to take up the slack. "I got into the National Guard along with the rest of the cops and jocks."

Everyone laughed but Dan. He left the fire ring and slipped into the dark. He was a long way from home, and it didn't seem like he was getting any closer.

He had never resented the various choices other people had been forced to make in response to the corrupt draft. He understood that everyone paid a price for whatever choices they made.

His service in Viet Nam had tested him in ways he had never imagined. He was proud of the work he had done. He didn't appreciate being judged as "stupid" by someone who only knew what they had been told on the evening news or in a movie.

He wondered what kind of person he would be now if he had stayed home; if he had lied or paid someone else to lie for him. He was pretty sure that was not the kind of person his parents had raised or that Lilly would respect or give her love to.

He found a place to sleep and scooped out the soft forest floor to accommodate his shoulders and hips.

"You got awful quiet." Scott had followed him from the fire. "Did that talk bother you?"

Dan looked at Scott in the dark and nodded. "Yeah," he paused and dug a pinecone out from under his sleeping bag. "Sometimes I wish I'd never come back here."

"You can't mean that."

Dan could see Scott's face in the light from the fire filtering through the trees. He didn't expect him, or anyone else, to understand.

"If it hadn't been for Lilly and my folks, Scott, I would have stayed in Viet Nam."

"You're kiddin' me."

"I never heard a baby cry, Scott. Think about it. In the middle of a war, I never heard a baby cry. The villagers never blamed me for the atrocities and the shit they took from us all day, every day. In my village there was no crime - there really was no crime. It seems to me they know something we don't."

Scott was listening but Dan could tell, he didn't get it.

He went on anyway, "People here think the vets are all fucked up because of the war. Well, that ain't all of it. Sure, the war is fucked up, but we have been goin' to war forever. We can handle that.

What really fucks us up now is the way we've been treated since we got back."

"Do you really believe that?"

"I do."

"I don't get it, Dan. The war seemed to be based on a bunch of lies. I sure didn't want to go."

Irritated by everything that had happened that evening he grunted, "Me neither, but I did. My great-grandfather carried the battle flag for the Wisconsin 13th in all four years of the Civil War."

Dan looked out over the dark outlines of the mountain wilderness then back at Scott.

"I guess he was a sort of hero to me. I still have his medals, stamped by hand. Guess I was just raised to do my duty, no matter what."

Scott grunted, lit his pipe, and handed it to Dan.

"Homegrown."

Dan hit the pipe and held the strong, sweet smoke.

"Thanks, man."

Scott went back to the fire. Dan slipped into his bag and sank into the welcome comfort of the earth.

Looking up, he embraced the stars framed by the treetops and tried to let the pot calm him. He finally fell asleep, waking up from time to time to note the progress of the constellations wheeling across the night sky.

## Chapter Thirteen

Thoughts of Suicide

Lilly was in her master's at Cal Poly, and he was excited to meet her for lunch at the Mexican food restaurant at the top of Monterey Street. Dan had never been suicidal, so he didn't see it coming when he stomped on the gas and yanked the wheel of the Sirocco at the line of on-coming cars in the other lane. He didn't think about it. Something snapped and he just did it.

Engine winding into a roar, he aimed at the cars on the other side. Suddenly confronted by the terror-stricken faces of the drivers he was about to hit head-on; Dan yanked the wheel back across the center line.

The driver's horrified faces slipped by. The sudden impulse to kill himself left as abruptly as it had arrived. The adrenalin drained from his body. He continued up Monterey Street to join Lilly for lunch.

They arrived at the same time. As she stepped out of her car, the impulse to destroy himself was swept away as her beauty washed over him.

He had heard about veterans killing themselves in single-car accidents. Dan was aware that more than four times as many veterans of Viet Nam had killed themselves since returning from the war than had died "in country." He never imagined he could be one of them.

Like when he was in the war, the moment passed. He survived it. He didn't die. He didn't even think about it until he tried to go to sleep that night and broke into a cold sweat. He could have been killed or injured or worse, could have killed or injured someone else.

But he hadn't. Like the rockets that had missed him, the threats on his life, the bombs that hadn't gone off, he survived it one more time. Like the rats, he tried to shrug it off - just one more thing to bury deep in his guts.

Lilly was asleep. He turned on his side, listening for the sound of the ocean, wishing it were morning, dreading the dreams he knew would come.

## Chapter Fourteen

Apples and Vigilantes

Dan leaned back in his chair and looked out the window at the lights of the city below in the soft light of dusk. How could a case that started out as felony attempted murder be plead down to a misdemeanor hit and run?

Phil stuck his head in, "You goin' home anytime soon?"

"Phil, tell me how the hell is a defendant charged with felony attempted murder allowed to enter a plea to misdemeanor hit and run?"

Phil shrugged and raised his eyebrows. "I need a ride to pick up my car. It's in the shop."

"What do you think about this?" Dan picked the incident report up off his desk.

Phil looked at his watch. "Beats me, Dan. What'd the D.A. say?"

"Nobody seems to know nothin.' I get a different D.A. and a different story every time I call."

"What about the police report?"

"The Highway Patrol's report is pretty straightforward. The defendant tried to hit one of his neighbors with his truck. It was on Los Berros Road, in front of witnesses, in broad daylight."

"What happened?"

"The victim, a Mr. Benito, was on Los Berros standing next to his pick-up talking to a neighbor when this guy, Russell, came down the road in his truck, swerved across the center line and rammed into the side of Benito's pick-up. He just missed him by inches."

Phil acted like he was interested, but Dan could see him looking at his wristwatch. Dan figured the mechanic would be closing up pretty soon and that he was Phil's last chance for a ride to pick up his car.

Dan tossed the police report on his desk and said, "Let's go get your car. I'll figure this out tomorrow."

But it wasn't that easy. The Highway Patrol got their arrest, and the D.A. got their conviction, such as it was. Obviously, the fix was in somewhere. But that didn't mean he had to go along with it.

Dan got to work late the next morning, and it wasn't long before his phone started ringing. The Defendant, Roland Russell, was on the phone.

"The clerk said I had to make an appointment with you for something called a pre-sentence report."

"Okay, when can you come in?"

"Can't we do it on the phone?"

"Not really."

"Why do I have to come talk to you?"

"You don't."

"What do you mean?"

"I'll just tell the judge you refused to make an appointment" Dan paused, "as ordered."

"Ordered? By whom?"

"The judge."

"Are you sure?"

"That's what the order says."

"Who the hell do you think you are?"

"I'm just the guy writing the report Mr. Russell and making the recommendation for sentencing."

"I entered a plea to reckless driving. So what?"

"Well, you still have to be sentenced, and I need to talk to you so I have some idea what to recommend."

"So, what are you going to recommend?"

"That's something we'll need to talk about when you come in."

Russell slammed down the phone.

Dan went to the men's room and washed his hands and face. When he got back to his desk the phone was ringing. It was Russell.

"What about tomorrow?"

"Let's make it Thursday at three."

"I'm a busy man."

"So am I."

Russell spit out, "Okay, Thursday at three."

Dan wrote it on his calendar, picked up the incident report, leaned back in the chair and put his feet up on the desk. Outside, two blackbirds were dive-bombing a red-tail hawk that had invaded the area around their nest.

This case didn't make any more sense this morning than it did last night.

He found the victim's number and dialed it. A young woman answered. When Dan explained what it was about, she said, "I can't talk to you about this right now. Let me talk to my husband and see what he says."

"Can I talk to him?"

"He's over at Mom and Dad's. We had a run-in with some of Russell's men today and they're pretty upset."

"What happened?"

"There's an easement at the back of the property and they came down here with their guns, yelling and cursing at us, calling us names, filthy names."

Dan didn't know what to say. She went on. "Mom's not well and this isn't making it any better. We had to call her doctor and take her in."

"Did you call the Sheriff?"

Silence. She took a deep breath and exhaled. "It doesn't do any good. They act like we're the problem. I think they're scared of him. They won't go up there."

She paused and went on. "The Sheriffs down here used to be great, but all the good ones have quit."

He felt some of the same helplessness he had known so often in Viet Nam. "When can we talk?"

"I'll let you know."

Dan gave her his number.

He was at his desk Thursday afternoon when the phone rang. It was the front desk.

"A Mr. Russell and another gentleman are here to see you."

"Have him fill out the questionnaire and I'll be right out."

"He won't fill it out."

"He refuses?"

"Right, he refuses."

"Okay." Dan hung up and walked down the long hall to the front desk.

Roland Russell was standing in the middle of the room holding the questionnaire in his hand like it was something distasteful.

He waved it in Dan's face yelling, "I'm not filling out this damn thing! I've got rights!"

"I understand," said Dan, picking up another questionnaire.

Russell turned to the other fellow who was dressed in an ill-fitting dark brown suit.

Russell pointed at him and almost shouted, "This is..." Dan didn't catch the name.

"He's running for the state Senate!"

Dan looked at the fellow standing behind Russell like he wished he were somewhere else.

"Is he your attorney?"

"No, he's my candidate!"

"Come on in, Mr. Russell."

Dan motioned toward his office.

They both started to follow him down the hall. He stopped and pointed at Russell, and said, "Just you, sir."

"He's with me. He needs to see this."

"Just you, Mr. Russell."

They walked back down the hall to Dan's office and sat down. Dan began filling out each line in the questionnaire.

"What kind of work do you do?"

"I'm self-employed."

Dan nodded and asked, "In what kind of work?"

"I provide housing for people who need it."

Dan waited.

"I own property. I rent."

"Income?"

"None of your damned business!"

Dan waited patiently, looking at Russell until he finally gave in.

"Fifty thousand give or take, actually, over fifty thousand. About fifty thousand a month."

Dan wrote it down.

Russell couldn't take it anymore and stood up muttering something about his rights as an American citizen.

"I'm leaving. You can't make me do this."

"That's up to you sir. I'll walk you out."

Dan escorted him to the front door and sat on the front steps while Russell collected his candidate for the state Senate, and drove away in his shiny, new Lincoln Town Car.

Dan went back to his office, closed the door, and wrote a short memo to the judge. He recommended that Russell be prohibited from any contact with the Benitos and given the maximum sentence the law would allow. He had a pretty good idea the judge would send the case back, which would give him some time to try to figure out what the heck was going on.

Mr. Benito's daughter-in-law finally called back.

"The family talked it over and we want to talk to you."

"Good. When can we meet?"

"We have to be careful. He tried to kill Dad. You know that, right?"

"It looks that way."

"Well, he hasn't given up."

Dan wasn't surprised. "I'll meet you, or whoever wants to talk to me at any time, any place."

"I was hoping you'd say that. You know where we live right?"

"I can find it."

"Okay, We're right off the south side of Los Berros Road. The houses are in a half circle with the apple orchard in the middle. Will you be in a county car?"

"Yes."

"I think it's better if nobody sees it."

"Okay, What time would be best for you?"

"What time does it get dark?"

"About seven."

"Can you come at eight-thirty tomorrow night?"

He thought about it, another late night.

"That'll be fine."

"It'd be best if you park your car in the orchard and turn out the lights. We'll come out."

Dan checked out a county car and drove down that morning so he could find the address in the dark. It was like the daughter-in-law had said. There was an apple orchard, with the little houses in a half-circle tucked up against the mesa. Just up the road was the location where Russell had tried to murder Mr. Benito.

When he got back to the office he called Lilly. "I have to work late tonight, Hon."

"Should I put the kids to bed?"

"Yeah," he sighed, "You better. This is going to be late, late. I'll tell you about it tomorrow, if you want."

She didn't say one way or the other. He knew the children were on her mind too. He paused. He knew Russell was dangerous and would try to come after him somehow. Still, he didn't want to worry her.

"Lilly?" He paused again, "Ah, how're the children?"

"They're fine."

He hated having to say it, "It's probably best to keep them out of the front yard for a while."

Her breath caught in her throat.

"I'm sorry, hon. I'm really sorry."

"Don't worry about it. I'll take care of it. They'll be fine."

"How about the front door?"

"I already locked it."

He could tell she was trying to be calm, but he could hear the anxiety in her voice.

"I'm sorry Lil."

"Dan?"

"Yeah?"

"I'm proud of you."

He took a deep breath. He didn't know what to say. He wasn't sure if he was proud of himself or not, or if that even had anything to do with it anymore.

He felt like he was bouncing downstream in a river flooded with the destruction of these people's lives and the community that had been his beloved home. He felt swept along, his mouth full of the bad taste of the greasy greed of one compromised case after another. With his feet frantically searching for a solid bottom, the shore kept flying by. But he couldn't see it because of the foul water in his mouth and eyes, the crisis of the next rapids roaring up fast.

He walked up the hill to the old Juvenile Hall and watched the sun go down. He watched the lights come on in the town that had been his home. He thought about the people who lived in those homes. Which ones were blind to what was going on? Which ones knew but chose to look the other way? Which ones were willing to go along to get along to further their own careers at the expense of others? Which ones were going to take it out on someone who couldn't protect themselves? Which ones were just trying to do the best they could? Which one was he?

He walked back down the hill and let himself in by the back door. The office was empty. He walked to the front desk and took the keys for one of the old Plymouths off its peg. The Plymouths liked to stall on a hard left turn, but they were quiet and didn't look like anything very official. He took his time cruising down 101, past Arroyo Grande and turned on to Los Berros Road. Everything *was* different in the dark.

He found the orchard, eased the car into the dirt driveway, turned off the lights, and idled in under the apple trees. Not wanting to be a target for any of Russell's men he turned off the dome light, rolled down the windows and sat in the dark listening for footsteps.

As his eyes adjusted to the dark, there was just enough starlight filtering through the trees to take notes. He knew that Benitos' little homes sat around the edge of the orchard, but he couldn't see them through the trees.

But they knew he was there, and it wasn't long before he heard someone coming. A young woman who must have been the daughter-in-law opened the passenger-side door and slipped into the car. She was a young mother in jeans and a work shirt with her hair pulled back into a tight ponytail. She didn't bother with introductions.

"What do you want to know about this mess?"

He recognized her voice from the phone.

"Just start at the beginning wherever that may be. It's best if you can keep it in some sort of chronological order, otherwise, I'll get confused and none of it will make sense."

She turned her head toward him, questioning.

He said, "Take your time." She started talking and he started writing. There was just enough light to see the page.

"Dad, grandpa, worked for the gas company all his life. This was his dream. It was our dream too. We pitched in everything we had and went together and bought this little orchard so we could all be together. We wanted to be close, like a family. We wanted our children to be close to Mom and Dad, and work together in the orchard, and have a little fruit stand where the children could sell the apples."

"It sounds wonderful."

"It was."

Dan noticed her use of the past tense and the sadness, and anger, in her voice.

"What happened?"

"Russell wanted our water."

"Your water?"

She nodded, pointing to the hills surrounding their acreage.

"That's the mesa up there. It flattens out on top. Russell bought all that land cheap but there's no water on it. He cut it up into an illegal subdivision with no water and no sewers so the workers from Diablo could park their campers and motorhomes up there. They all had money, but nowhere to live."

"What about the county? The Planning Department? Code Enforcement?"

"They're afraid to go in there. They tried once but got run off. All those guys have guns, lots of guns. Russell has his own little army of thugs. They say it's 'to keep the peace.'"

Dan was taking notes as fast as he could. She stopped to let him catch up.

"There never has been any water up there. Everyone knew that, but he came in here with lots of money from somewhere back east and thought he knew better. When he didn't find water, he decided to take ours. We have water here." She pointed to the trees, silent in the dark, "and he wanted it."

"He tried to buy us out, but this was our dream, three generations, together, like it should be. We have the apples, and bees, and honey too. We help each other out with everything. The kids get to play with their cousins every day and best of all they learn how to work and live together."

"So, he tried to kill your father-in-law?"

"He'd tried everything else to get the water. He was mad and frustrated."

She turned and looked at Dan. "One thing you need to know about Russell. He believes he's above the law."

"I can see that."

She looked at him again, this time with a little bit of hope.

"I just pray that he pays for what he's done to our family. When Lorenzo and I were married they took me in and treated me like their own. I never had a family like that."

She stopped and looked at Dan in the dark. "Thank you for listening to us."

She slipped out of the car and was gone.

Dan sat in the dark and waited. He heard another person coming through the orchard. A man opened the door, got into the car, and slowly pulled the door closed to the first click.

"I'm Lorenzo."

They shook hands.

Dan said, "Tell me what's going on here."

Lorenzo was quiet, but clearly upset. He stared out at the trees and sighed, "She told you about Russell?"

"Uh-huh." Dan waited.

"Well, they sabotaged our pump. They ran wires with two hundred and twenty volts from the electric box to the pump handle so whoever turned it on could get electrocuted."

"Anybody get hurt?"

"No, we saw it in time and disconnected the wires, but if we'd tried to turn on the pump, who knows, we might have been fried."

"Another thing they did was to flood the orchard with our own water. Then they ran two-twenty wires from the electrical box into the water."

"What happened with that?"

"Luckily, we saw the wires and kept everyone out of the orchard. I called a friend of mine who's an electrician. He came over and looked at it and turned off the juice. He said it was an amateur job, but you never know. If they were trying to scare us, it worked."

He paused, giving Dan time to catch up.

"We can't even let the kids out of the house to play now. We never know what they are going to do next."

"Did you call the Sheriff?"

Lorenzo sat in the dark shaking his head. "The Sheriff won't do anything out here."

He turned and looked at Dan. "You should know that things have gotten so bad that the people out here in the Los Berros have put together a group, a sorta vigilante committee."

"Vigilante Committee?"

Dan remembered reading about the Vigilante Committee of 1858. He realized that things must be worse out here than anybody was willing to acknowledge.

He asked, "How come?"

"To protect ourselves. The new sheriff won't do anything, you know, since they started construction at Diablo. All the good deputies have quit. The rest are a bunch of drunks."

Lorenzo paused to catch his breath then went on.

"You know how it works. The County hired a drunk for a Sheriff. The deputies follow his lead. The people who rent from Russell all work out at the power plant. They got a lot of money and they're buying the drinks."

"Are you, your family, on the committee?"

"No," Lorenzo was adamant. "When this happened, they thought we would join 'em. My brother and I talked to our father about it. He said, 'No, this is our country, and this is our land. We will obey the law and only the law.'"

"Even when the law lets you down?"

Lorenzo put his head between his hands, pushing back his hair.

"We've talked about it." He stopped and took a deep breath. "My father says it doesn't matter. His family will obey the law. We're gonna do as he says."

Dan looked out the window at the comforting regular shapes of the apple trees in the dark.

Lorenzo asked him, "Can you help us, my mom and dad?"

"I don't know what's gonna happen with this, Lorenzo. I'll do what I can."

Lorenzo sat up, looked Dan in the eye and shook his hand.

"That's all anybody can do."

The others came out of their little houses one by one telling more of the same story. By the time they were done Grandpa and Grandma Benito had gone to bed and Dan had half a legal tablet of notes.

. . .

When the case went back to court for sentencing the judge had read Dan's memo regarding Russell's refusal to cooperate for the interview. The Judge impressed upon Russell the importance of the report and sent him back for another interview.

The phone rang and it was the front desk.

"A Mr. Russell is here to see you.

"I'll be right out."

"Do you want him to fill out the questionnaire?"

"We got one the other day, thanks."

Russell's wife and daughter were with him. Expensive clothes, perfect hair and makeup, disgusted with being there among the "riffraff". They sat on each side of Russell glaring at Dan with contempt. He walked Russell to his office, closed the door, and sat down at his desk.

"Well, what are you going to recommend?" Russell demanded.

"I'm going to recommend that you go to jail and leave the Benitos alone."

"Jail!" Russell stood up yelling, "Who the hell do you think you are? You're in deep shit young man!"

"Is that a threat?"

Russell shut up and sat down.

Dan asked him about his past relationship with Mr. Benito, and Russell blew up again. Jumping back to his feet, he shook his finger and glared at Dan yelling, "The next time I'll get that son-of-a-bitch!"

Dan wrote it down exactly like he said it. Russell was still on his feet, huffing and puffing. Dan checked his notes one more time and then stood up saying, "You can go now."

Russell shut up, then blurted out, "What do you mean? Don't you want to ask me about my family or anything?"

"I think I know enough," Dan said looking at his notes where Russell had said "The next time I'll get that son-of-a-bitch." That was pretty much all he needed to know.

Dan had made it a practice to never question the court's decisions. On intake cases like this he rarely, if ever, checked to see if the judge had followed his recommendations. He figured the judge knew more than he did, or at least was getting paid more than he was. Besides, there were more cases filling up his drawer every day.

But this case stunk. The Benitos had put their faith in the law and the law had let them down. His report had eight legal-sized pages of the statements the Benitos had given him that night in the apple orchard. It also had Mr. Russell's statement that "the next time he would get the son-of-a-bitch!"

He finished the report with the recommendation that Russell be fined the maximum, sentenced to the maximum time in jail, and forbidden from having contact of any kind with the Benitos, or their property.

It had already been reduced to a misdemeanor and Dan wanted to make sure it didn't go sideways any farther. He put on his sport coat and the tie Lilly had given him for luck and went to court.

The little courtroom in Grover City was crowded and Mr. Russell's squad of expensive attorneys pushed to the head of the morning calendar. Russell and his wife and daughter sat glaring at Dan who was standing along the side.

Russell's attorneys demanded that the hearing be transferred to San Luis Obispo, which the Judge was happy to grant. Russell, along with his wife, daughter, and attorneys, swept out of the courtroom like they had won the case.

"What did the Judge say?" Mr. Benito asked, leaning close to Dan.

"He transferred the case to San Luis."

"Why did he do that?"

Dan looked at him and said, "I don't know."

"When will it be?"

"This afternoon at one-thirty."

"Will you be there?"

"Yes."

"Then we will go there, too."

"Do you know where the courthouse is?"

"Across the street from the movie?"

Dan nodded and said, "I'll meet you there."

Reynolds was the D.A. He nodded at Dan and addressed the court.

"Your Honor, the victims, Mr. and Mrs. Benito are present in court along with the investigating Probation Officer."

Out of the corner of his eye, Dan could see the Benitos, sitting together in the back of the courtroom, waiting patiently for justice.

But the case was continued and continued again, keeping Mr. Russell out of jail for the time being. He hired and fired one attorney after another. They all complained bitterly about the "unfair and prejudicial" victim statements in Dan's report. Weeks went by and the case was not resolved, and Russell was still not sentenced. Finally, it was set for sentencing back in the Grover court.

Dan called the D.A. This time it was a young woman.

"I like your report, Dan. Let's stop fooling around with this thing."

Dan asked, "Can you get the jail time? Mr. Russell does not want to go to jail, even for a minute."

"I think we can. The judge is fed up with him and his pals."

"His pals?"

"Yeah, they've formed some sort of 'free Americans we won't pay taxes' group. There's a bunch of them out there on the mesa. They forced one of our best young D.A.s to resign."

"You're kidding."

"Not at all. They tried all kinds of things to break him. One time they ordered truckloads of gravel to be dumped in his driveway. Imagine coming home to that."

"Another time they ordered a big load of irrigation pipe delivered to his house. Finally, they ran him off the road on the way to Santa Maria. When he got out of the hospital he resigned. It doesn't look like he will ever recover from his injuries or practice law again."

Dan made sure he went to the sentencing hearing in Grover. The courtroom was full. Russell and his wife and daughter glared at him. The back of the room was lined with Russell's friends standing against the back wall. They were talking and laughing, generally showing their disrespect for the court and everyone in it. Mr. and Mrs. Benito nodded at Dan from their seat four rows back.

Dan approached the bench. The defense attorneys were in a pack on the right and the D.A. was on the left by herself. She looked small and alone, busily shuffling cases and stacks of papers.

Dan introduced himself.

She looked up and smiled like this was the most fun ever.

"Hi, I'm Cate. We talked, right?"

"Yeah." He could see she wasn't in the least bit intimidated. She raised her eyebrows and whispered, "Glad you made it."

"All rise," the bailiff called as the judge walked in, gathered his robes around himself and sat down.

The "Don't Tread on Me" bunch in the back guffawed and shuffled their feet. The bailiff watched them without expression.

Judge Daniels was a big man with a full head of thick black hair and black eyebrows. He took his time, waiting until the courtroom was still. Then he waited a little longer, leaning forward from the bench, looking at each one of the men in the back row. Dan knew that some of these men were the judge's friends, members of the same churches, the same clubs, men who had voted for him when he ran for the judgeship.

He waited until he had their full attention, and the courtroom was quiet, then said, "This stops now." He didn't especially raise his voice, but it was loud and clear. "You all know what I'm talking about. This is the end of it."

The "Don't Tread on Me" bunch in the back row glared at him and opened their mouths to express their sense of outrage.

The Judge cut them off, "Whether you agree or disagree is of no consequence to this court."

He stopped and looked up and down the line of men. "From now on you're dealing with me."

Nobody spoke - nobody moved. He turned to the clerk and said, "First case, please."

As usual, Russell's attorneys had pushed their way to the front of the calendar. Judge Daniels let them wait, taking the other private attorneys first and then the Public Defenders.

By the time Russell's case was called the courtroom was empty and his friends in the back row were gone.

Cate introduced the case, "Your Honor, this is the matter of Roland Russell appearing for sentencing on a charge of reckless driving. His counsel is present along with the investigating Probation Officer and the victim, Mr. Benito."

The Judge acknowledged the Benitos and nodded at Dan.

One of Russell's attorneys opened by protesting the eight pages of the Victim's Statement.

"Your Honor, this report ... "

Judge Daniels leaned forward and looked at him through his thick eyebrows.

The attorney stammered, stopped, took a breath, and started over. "We believe this report is weighted in favor of the victim."

The Judge stopped him. "Duly noted." He paused and stared at Russell's attorney. "Any other reason why sentencing should not proceed?"

Russell looked around the empty courtroom.

Cate said, "No, Your Honor."

The Judge turned to the recommendation page. "Mr. Russell, you are ordered to have no contact of any kind with Mr. and Mrs. Benito, or any member of their family. You are ordered to pay restitution for the damages to Mr. Benito's pick-up when you ran into it, and you are ordered to pay the maximum fine allowed under the law. Do you understand?"

Russell nodded. The Judge waited. Russell finally grunted, "Yeah."

"And you are now remanded into the custody of the Sheriff's Department for the maximum time allowed by law."

Mrs. Russell gasped. The daughter wheeled around and gave Dan a dirty, dirty look.

The Bailiff stepped forward. Russell was still defiant but speechless. The Bailiff snapped the handcuffs around his wrists.

Dan stepped forward and said, "Thank you, Your Honor."

The Judge nodded.

Dan leaned over Cate's shoulder and whispered, "Thanks!"

She grinned, nodded, and reached for her next case.

He met the Benitos outside. The flag was snapping in the stiff ocean breeze, the rope banging against the steel pole.

"I'm sorry this took so long," Dan said.

Mr. Benito shook his hand, "We knew it wouldn't be easy. We're just grateful someone listened to us." There was a silence, then he went on. "At least he's stopped harassing us for now."

Dan was surprised, "Really? Good."

"He's been leaving us alone ever since the first time we went to court. We've heard he's putting his properties up for sale and going back to where he came from."

Dan said, "I'm glad he's not bothering you and your family."

Mr. Benito took Dan's hand and said, "We are too. Thank you."

Mrs. Benito leaned around her husband and said with a big smile, "But he sure is mad at you!"

Dan laughed. If a guy like Russell hated him, he must be doing something right.

## Chapter Fifteen

### Jail Program

Dan stood with his back against the cold concrete block wall of the jail and realized that this was where he was supposed to be all along.

He thought back to when he had been selected from more than two hundred and fifty applicants for this job as a Probation Officer. He always tested well, but nonetheless, he was surprised when he was actually hired.

They had told him, "Just get a haircut."

He had only been back from Viet Nam for a year or so, but Lilly had brought them the miracle of a newborn daughter and he needed a job with better pay. So, he took the test and was offered the job. *Just get a haircut.* He'd had enough of haircuts and taking orders. It was the early 1970's and along with beards, mustaches, and sideburns, men were wearing their hair longer. So, he turned the job down, shook hands all around and walked out of the hiring interview.

It wasn't that he really cared about his hair. But he'd had enough of the blind bigotry in the military. He remembered his commanding officer saying *"I ain't gonna talk to no gook"*, when the village elders had come to Dan with their offer to work with his command. After months of putting his life on the line every day, he and the corpsmen had *Won the Peace* in that small corner of the war. But it had been all thrown away because his commanding officer wasn't going to *talk to no gook?*

He remembered tearing the commander's office apart in his anger, then walking off the base and going absent without leave, back to the village, ashamed. Ashamed of himself, ashamed of his command, ashamed of his country and ashamed of his race.

What could he ever say to the elders, these wise gentlemen who had trusted and protected him, offered him tea and affection without fail.

He'd had enough bigotry for more than one lifetime. But now he had a wife and a daughter and another child coming, so this was about them, and his responsibility to provide and care for them.

So, when a couple of weeks later they called him back and offered him the job, he took it. All they said was, "Get a haircut and you got the job."

No problem. His responsibilities to Lilly and the baby outweighed any misgivings he might have had about a haircut. Lilly didn't care for the mustache, and he didn't look especially good with long hair anyway. At the same time, he couldn't help but wonder about what was so wrong with the two hundred and fifty other applicants.

At the end of his first six months, his evaluation had stated that he was "a square peg in a round hole." Even though he tried to take it as a compliment, he knew it was true and that led back to the question of why he had been chosen for this job in the first place.

He wondered about it for years. He felt trapped, prayed about it, and talked to Lilly and his father about it. He twisted and turned and looked for other work. He finally considered that for better or worse, it had to be the "Big Boot of Providence" pushing him along to where he was supposed to be.

Even though he loved the work, he knew that he remained that square peg that never quite fit.

While his experiences in Viet Nam had certainly prepared him to stand on his own feet, he had hoped for a place where he could do his duty and contribute to his community without spending the rest of his days in conflict with the world around him. It was not to be.

Time passed with no change. He found himself at odds in an environment where his peers said, "Go along to get along" with a smirk and didn't see anything wrong with it. He saw weak people look the other way, blind to the consequences of their actions. But he also saw good people do their very best to do their duty every day and they inspired him to continue.

Lilly bore them a daughter and then a son. He was blessed at home and loved his work, but he was still that square peg. He prayed about going to work somewhere else.

*Please show me the way. Open a door. Please place my foot on the path.* The door to this job had certainly been open when he was hired, but now it was slammed shut. He wasn't going anywhere. San Luis Obispo was his home.

More time passed. No change. He still loved the work. It came easy to him. He earned a master's degree that gave him insight, tools and the ability to meet the challenges of increasingly difficult cases. But it didn't matter. He was still that square peg.

He had been raised by parents whose lives were grounded in the rich, black soil of the Midwest. They were people who worked long, hard hours all week and took satisfaction in doing honest work. They went to church on Sunday where his father sometimes fell asleep sitting upright in the pew.

He thought about his great-grandfather who had carried the Battle Flag of the Wisconsin 13th Infantry through all four years of the American Civil War.

During the day Dan forgot about the rats he still held in his belly. But at night when he tried to sleep they came for his eyes.

He sometimes imagined himself as a rough chunk of the Big Sur jade grinding away in the surge of the surf, knocking off the soapstone, smoothing the sharp edges a little bit at a time. He hoped he could be like that kind of smooth stone, but had a pretty good idea it was not going to happen, at least not in this lifetime. He couldn't change if he wanted to.

Lilly told him, "Don't try to be something you're not. It only makes it worse."

He asked, "You mean like with your mother?"

She gave him "the look" and then laughed, "*Exactly* like with my mother. Just be yourself."

Then he went to jail, and everything changed.

## Chapter Sixteen

### In the Belly of the Beast

Tommy, his Division Manager, had approached him and said, "We need someone to represent the Department at the Jail Counseling meeting. The Medical, Mental Health, Drug and Alcohol and AA volunteers meet once a month to coordinate their services. We need someone from Probation to attend the meeting. What do you think?"

"You want me to do it?"

Tommy smiled and nodded. Dan knew Tommy's plate was full. He also knew that most of the officers were unwilling to go to the jail and figured no one else would do it.

"Sure, I'll do it, Tom."

So, he went to jail. Dan was impressed with the staff's competence and willingness to provide care in such a difficult, often overwhelming, environment. He was also impressed with the majority of the Correctional Officers who seemed to be genuinely concerned for the men and women in their care.

After a couple of months, Caroline, the lady representing Drug and Alcohol Services in the jail, asked him if he would like to join her in a Men's Group she conducted once a week in the classroom.

She said, "I could use the help, and I think the men would benefit from having a man, especially a probation officer, in the group. They have so many questions about the system."

He said, "Sure, I'd be happy to."

They had met in the jail's classroom for several months when the new wing of the jail opened.

Caroline called him, "We won't have the classroom anymore."

"How come?"

"They opened the new wing on the jail and don't have the staff to round up the guys, bring them over, then take them back before count."

The group in the classroom had been working well and Dan could sense that she was not too happy with the change. Neither was he.

She continued, "What they've done is put all the guys who are in some sort of treatment, you know, AA or Drug and Alcohol, or whatever, into one of the new units. The Correctional Officers said we can have our groups over there, in the unit with the men."

This was outside the comfort zone for both of them. Meeting in her office she said, "I kind of liked it the way it was. It was working."

Dan agreed. "So, what do we do?"

She shrugged, "Maybe it's time for *us* to make a change."

The unit was shaped like a piece of a pie with individual rooms along one side. The wide front section was all glass. The men were sitting around a big table, watching him and Caroline walk down the hall and stop in front of the glass door.

The Correctional Officer above in the central office pushed the button and the solenoid unlocked the door with a loud "click."

This was it. They stepped into the big, new room and the door clunked closed behind them. Four old shot callers who had been in the system for most of their lives sat across the big table from each other, two on each side. The rest of the men sat around the table facing the door. Two chairs at the end closest to the door had been left empty for Caroline and Dan. They sat down and looked around at the group of men. No one spoke.

Finally, one of the shot callers looked at them and said, "We've been talking. There's no treatment in the joint. There never has been. They say there is, but there isn't, not really. Something's got to give."

The men around the table all nodded in silent agreement.

The shot caller went on, "We've been having our AA meetings every morning and every night. We've been praying, praying hard on this, all of us."

He stopped and looked around the table. The men all nodded their agreement.

He continued, "This program is the answer to our prayers."

Dan looked around the group. Scars, tattoos, hearts, and spirits tattered and worn, eyes that had seen too much. Each man nodded in turn.

He didn't know what to say. Program? What program? A program based on their prayers? No grant? No big interagency budget battles? It just happened because of the prayers of these forgotten, forsaken men?

He looked at Caroline. Like Dan, she was listening. He could feel the Correctional Officers watching through the glass.

Starting with the two leaders on Dan's left, they went around the table, each man telling about his needs, his hopeless history, his unyielding sense of isolation and loneliness, his desperate desire for something better. The two leaders on Dan's right asked, "Are you in? Will you help us?"

Dan was moved. These men reminded him of himself. He could not escape the feeling that he was witnessing a miracle of the spirit. He looked around the group of men who were waiting for his response. His nod of consent was barely perceptible but they knew he was in.

After group, Dan stood with his back against the cold concrete wall of the jail and knew this was where he was supposed to be all along. He realized this was why he had been chosen over so many other applicants for the job. He understood that this program is why his prayers for a different job had never been answered. Now they had been. At last, he knew why the square peg in the round hole had been held here in the bowels of the system for so long.

Months later, when he brought it up in group, the men in the program told him, "God's time is not our time."

He knew he was different from the other probation officers. In many ways, he felt more in common with the men in the group than with his own peers. He *was* that square peg in the round hole. So were they. They had a saying:

> *Don't lead, I may not follow.*
>
> *Don't follow, I may not lead.*
>
> *Walk beside me and be my friend.*

## Chapter Seventeen

### Anniversary Dates

Dan got a call from his friend David, another vet.

"Remember Charlie?" David asked.

"Don't think so."

"Yeah, we met him at that coffee shop one time. He lives over there by you. The front yard has a rock wall and a steel gate."

Dan remembered. Charlie was short and heavy, sweaty and intense.

"His anniversary date is coming up in a few days."

Dan grunted. He didn't need this right now.

David went on, "We're putting together a list of guys he can talk to for the next few days."

"How's he doin'?"

"Not too good Dan. He needs to talk... to us, other vets. He won't talk to anyone else. If they bring the cops in, it'll be a mess. We gotta keep him talking 'til he gets through it."

"When's his anniversary date?"

"About two more days. He's not sleepin' Dan. He's the sole survivor of a company of a hundred and fifty men."

Dan held the phone to his ear and closed his eyes.

"He went back and found 'em dead with their weapons jammed."

"Fuckin' Army and their hot rounds."

"Yeah, and every night now, coming up to his anniversary date, he sees every one of them in his dreams."

"All hundred and fifty?"

"Everyone of 'em."

"What's he doing now?"

"Sittin' at the kitchen table with his guns and knives, drinking vodka from the bottle."

"Shit."

"Yeah. He ran off the wife and kids."

"They okay?"

"Far as I know. They had a pretty good idea when to get outta' there. He goes through this every year. She said he's booby-trapped the doors and the front gate. She's afraid to go back."

"Damn it, what's the number?"

David gave it to him. Charlie picked up on the first ring. He didn't say anything. Dan could hear a smooth scratching sound - *schniiick, schniiick, schniiick.* Steel on stone. Charlie sitting in the dark, sharpening his K-Bar.

"Hey, Charlie."

"Hey," his voice was flat.

Silence. The sound stopped. Dan could tell he was testing the knife's edge.

"Charlie."

"Yeah."

"This is Dan. David asked me to give you a call."

"You a vet?"

"Yeah."

"Were you in 'Nam?"

"I was."

"...K."

Dan heard the sound again, steel on stone, smooth, even strokes, *schniiick, schniiick*.

Everything he could think of saying sounded stupid. He waited.

"You a vet?" Charlie asked again.

"Yeah."

"What year?"

"Sixty-eight, sixty-nine."

A long silence then he said, "I see their faces man, every one of 'em."

His voice was without emotion of any kind.

"They come to me in a long line when I close my eyes. The whole fuckin' company, I see 'em all, even the guys I didn't know, the new guys. I see their faces. They just keep on comin', one after the other, over and over again. It fucks me up. They say it will get better with time. It don't. They say the meds will help. They don't. It gets worse every fuckin' year."

There was a long silence. Finally, Charlie said. "I just gotta' keep my eyes open for the next couple of days. I just want it to stop."

Sitting at the kitchen table, Dan cradled his head in his arms while keeping the phone to his ear. The children were asleep and Lilly had left the room.

He wanted to ask Charlie if he was okay, but he knew he wasn't. He just waited, listening, keeping the line open. The sound of the knife, steel on stone, dressing one side after the other, seemed like it would never stop.

## Chapter Eighteen

### Red Wind

Dan had been invited to a birthday celebration at Red Wind, a settlement of First Nation individuals who had created a small community in the National Forest lands east of Santa Margarita. His guide that day was Salvador, a young man of Native American heritage, who had started work alongside Dan at Probation.

Bumping along on the dirt road Sal explained, "It's Grandfather's birthday."

"Grandfather?"

Sal looked at him and grinned, "Yeah, Grandfather. Red Wind was his vision."

The land was dry, rock and sand, scattered brush with a few sad pines. The air was thin and hot. Sal drove carefully as the rough, dirt road dropped down along the side of a steep ridge then circled below and around into a meadow. In the meadow was an Indian village. The round wooden buildings had been carefully crafted to pay homage

— 142 —

to the grace and beauty of the buffalo skin lodges of the plains. With no corners, every space had a special purpose.

In the center of the meadow was a Kiva. Also built in a circle, it was mostly below ground where it was cool in the heat of the day. The small part above ground had been carefully fitted with slots, or windows, to catch the rays of the rising and setting sun and moon during what we call the solstice and what they called the four paths, or ways of being. Dan wanted to stay there forever, but he understood it was their holy place and felt honored that they had allowed him to enter it, if only for a moment.

He and Sal joined a mixed group of residents and visitors on a trail along a dry creek until they came to a pool of standing water seeping through the rocks. The trail left the creek and climbed up and up to the top of a hill where an old man and old woman sat on a blanket in the shade of a big pine tree.

When everyone had found a seat on the ground, the elders told the story of Red Wind.

"Many of our people were in the white man's jail. Many of them were using alcohol and drugs. Many of the children had no one to teach them the ways of their people. Grandfather heard their cries and came here, to this land. He built a fire. He offered his prayers to the father above and mother below. He waited and the people came. One by one they came and joined him. They had no place else to go. They dug the wells and built the buildings to honor each and every nation, every tribe, every people, and more and more came.

"The authorities said, 'You cannot build here! You cannot live here!' The Sheriff came out and said, 'You have to leave! You cannot live here!'

Then he went away.

It's Grandfather's vision. It's our dream. We live in the old ways, and here we are."

While Dan listened, he noticed the red ants busily running in and out of their ant world. He looked up and saw that the old woman was watching him and the ants. Almost embarrassed, he took note of her face while she nodded and pursed her lips to keep from smiling.

While he was watching she rose, left the group, and returned with a large mixing bowl in both hands. The old man cleared away the embers remaining from the fire and brushed the ground clean. Once the ground was prepared, the woman poured what looked like corn meal onto the still warm earth, and the man began to tell a story.

"A group of warriors had fared poorly on a raid. Not only had they failed to take horses or captives, they had also suffered losses of their own. One man was killed, and they were unable to recover his body. Two were seriously wounded, and their horses killed beneath them. They were forced to ride double while making their escape.

"Now, one of the wounded had fallen from the horse's back and was drawn into a ball on the ground, moaning 'Go on my brothers! Leave me here and make your escape. I can hear the hoofs of our enemies beating the ground as they approach.'

"The group's leader said, 'We cannot leave you. Get on the horse!'

'I cannot. I have not the strength.'

"There was a holy man with the group. He dismounted and approached the wounded one."

'Get up my brother, get up!'

'I cannot.'

"The holy man returned to his mount and removed a long horse-hide whip. With the whip, he approached the man on the ground and struck the earth, *Crack!* first one side then the other, *Crack!* The whip struck first the earth, then the air above the wounded man, again and again, closer and closer, louder and louder. And all the time the holy man was chanting louder and louder, 'Get up, get up! Your brothers need you.' When he did not respond the holy man began cursing him in the worst possible language and all the time the whip was coming closer and closer to the wounded man until it was right in his ears and in his face.

"All at once he gasped and looked around as if he had come out of a dream. He arose from the ground and struggled to his feet. He mounted the horse behind his comrade and one by one, in single file they slipped away into the night."

The elder stopped then and the people in the circle sat in silence watching the corn meal change into bread.

When it was ready, the elder cut the bread into four directions and offered it to the group. When everyone had been given a piece of bread one of the young women asked, "What happened? Did they make it home?"

The elder looked at the old woman who was watching the ants systematically dismantle what was left of the bread for their own use. Becoming aware of his gaze she smiled and lifted her eyes to the circle of listeners.

She looked around the group and began to tell the rest of the story.

"So, everyone in the village was waiting for their return. It had been long overdue and their hearts were burdened with worry. The raiding party was injured in body and spirit. They approached the village slowly, some riding tired and injured horses, some riding double and some walking with their eyes on the ground.

"They ate and rested while the people prepared a feast and a fire. That evening the drums drummed and the people danced around the fire while the returning warriors each told their story in song. Not all the stories were filled with honor, or even bravery. The raid had gone poorly, and they told of having to flee, to accept the disgrace of leaving the one behind and not bring his body home to be grieved and prepared for burial by his loved ones. The women cried and cut themselves to show their grief while some trilled and sang to show their grief and sadness but not to blame the men who had returned.

"The drumming and the songs went on until each man's story was told and he was empty of his grief and shame. Finally, as the fire burned down, each warrior once again became the father, husband, brother, and sweetheart they had once been, and returned to sleep in the lodge where they belonged."

Dan thought of Charlie, the poor tortured veteran of Viet Nam, sharpening his knife, while drinking vodka from the bottle, overcome by his dread of seeing every one of the faces - the souls - of his murdered comrades who would come to him in his dreams when he tried to sleep. What if his poor soul could have been welcomed to the drums, the fire, the dance of *his* people, instead of being cast out to wander forever, in that strange land between this life and the next?

Now, at Red Wind, the drumming started just as the sun slid behind the dark shadow of the Sierra Madre. The fire had been set in the center of the meadow and Dan watched spellbound as the flames rose to join the reds and oranges of the fading sunset in the western sky.

The drums beat louder and louder in time to the leaping flames urging them on, higher and higher into the night sky. The dancers appeared, dark silhouettes around the fire, strange figures with ancient, timeless gestures.

The drumming filled his bones. The light from the fire filled his eyes. The motions of the dancers filled his senses. Past and present became one and the same. He sat with his ancestors among the peoples of the forests and the plains and the mountains in this land before time.

# Chapter Nineteen

## The Hourglass and the Tao

He wished he could go back to sit on the veranda with Ong De and once more seek his wisdom. He remembered the way Ong De had made the sign for infinity with two circles crossing then being folded over to make the symbol of the Tao with two sides, and then saying, "but where the *center is always gently balancing one with the other,* always changing, always creating love and growth within the universe and within each one of us as well."

He remembered the hourglass where he had seen himself suspended upside down until all his beliefs of western civilization had drained out on the ground and he had realized that the beliefs of the East were not just different from those of the West but indeed the *opposite.*

Where, why had he lost that wisdom? Had he ever really believed it, or was it just another notion buried beneath the unrelenting avalanche of movies, books and non-stop commercials dedicated to the certain belief of an eternal struggle between good and evil, male and female, rich and poor, black and white, life and death? Even self against self, especially self against self.

Ong De, my friend, and teacher, where are you now?

# Chapter Twenty

## De La Cruz

The tongue of swirling water – the last of the edge of a breaking wave, now almost spent, reached out and tugged at his ankle and ran away, asking, "Why are you here on this lonely beach?"

He walked splashing through the shallowing surf watching the exploding showers of diamonds catching the light, then disappearing and gone forever. One step followed another until all that was left was a few lost bubbles and the last of the wave sheeting back over the smooth sand, hurrying to catch up, whispering, "wait for me."

The next wave built silently and for the moment he was alone. It broke far up the beach then curled around him and finally collapsed in one piece with an explosion of sound heard around the world on this and every shore.

The wave's tongue didn't quite reach the spot of sand where he now stood. He watched it slide toward him, then fall away. He wondered if these drops of water had this same duty all day, every day, or did they rotate, changing places with the water from somewhere cooler, or warmer, some other shore.

He thought about the warm water of the South China Sea, too warm to even be refreshing. He had made his way to that coast whenever he could and taken to the water to relieve the heat rash. He believed the ocean was good for everything, a cure for every ill. Maybe it was. At least it did no harm.

Now he came to this place on the beach and sat with his back against the bluff of the ancient Indian village watching the swells of the open ocean marching across the curve of the horizon.

He stood and imagined the earth rotating beneath his feet and thought, *the earth's a splendid ball spinning a thousand miles an hour.*

And he felt it lurch and push him off balance then lurch again and go on as before. Looking over the horizon, he thought, *while it's spinning a thousand miles an hour it's flying around the sun even faster. And the sun on its journey pulls us along as it goes.* And he felt the lightness of it pulling him along.

And he thought, *we are all spinning, flying, flung into some strange pattern we cannot comprehend to somewhere we cannot imagine.*

And while he took notice of his tiny place in it all, the biggest wave in the set crashed with a roar on the beach and rushed toward him. Slowed by the rocks and gravel, the white foam washed over the sandbar whispering to him as it sank into the sand.

Just before dawn the next morning, he slipped out of his sleeping bag and stood for a moment looking across the still water of the lagoon. The light of the coming day in the sky above, shone reflected in the smooth surface of the water below.

As he walked along the shore, he could see the willows on the north side of the lagoon where the water was deepest. The spirit of the place stood on the water looking at him. It seemed to say, "*I see you.*"

They remained looking at each other across the water until he was certain that what he was seeing was not an illusion but as real as the sand and the rocks and sea. He went back to the camp and sought the warmth of his bed in the sand. Listening to the sound of the waves on the shore he had just dozed off when he felt a lurch through the sand and the gears of the earth caught, and turned, and turned again.

The End

*I have no religion - everything is sacred.*

## Epilogue

### Penelope

Against all odds, the manuscript of "One Day in the Village" found a publisher and shortly thereafter Lilly and Dan began attending book signings in the community. Dan felt gratified and humbled by the overwhelmingly positive response from the readers. Their thoughtful questions and comments broadened, challenged, and often validated, his own understanding of what he had struggled to squeeze out of the words on the pages.

One of the readers' groups was held in a second-story conference room south of San Luis Obispo where the generous windows opened east to peaceful views of the timeless Sierra Madre.

The presentation began with brief introductions from the members of the group who sat almost in silhouette with their backs to the windows. They shared how long they had lived in San Luis Obispo and for how long they had been part of the group. Some had been present for many years and some for only a few. As the introductions went around the room Dan began to feel he had met them all before.

On the way home Dan turned to Lilly and said, "I never really anticipated all those questions. They took me to the wall, over and over again. Not only had they read the book, but they also seemed to grasp what I was trying to say."

She smiled at him and said, "You might want to keep track of the questions. It could be another book."

Dan was thrilled and at the same time exhausted. He slept through the night for the first time since the nightmares had begun so many years ago. As the light of a new day filtered through the trees, he opened his eyes to a feeling of peacefulness.

Downstairs, he could hear Lilly making coffee with its rich smell, the promise of a new day. The top of his head tingled, and he imagined the two sides of his brain at long last mingling in a strange dance of molecular joy. He descended the stairs rubbing the top of his head wondering if his hair had curled while he slept.

Still rubbing his head, he took a chair at the breakfast table as if it were the first time. The morning light streamed through the windows. Lilly's smile filled the room with gold.

Awash in her beauty, he said, "I feel like I've finally made it home, Lil. Do I look different?"

She shrugged, "Kind of, in a way."

"I feel so good," he paused trying to put his feelings into words, "Like I am all in one piece." He paused again. "I never want to lose the way I feel right now."

She looked at him and raised her eyebrows in a smile but didn't say anything.

Something in her silence brought the story of Penelope to his mind. Lilly's letters to him every day reminded him of the years that Penelope had resisted the demands of the suitors while Odysseus was trapped by the gods to roam the ancient world.

All at once Dan grasped the weight of the burden Lilly had carried for so long without complaint. Staggered by the cost of her sacrifice, he gasped, "It has been so long for you as well, hasn't it?"

She nodded, tried to force a smile, then said, "I am happy for you, Dan. I'm really happy you feel like you're finally home."

She stopped and took a breath, letting it out slowly, "And yes, it has been a long time for me also."

He sat at the table with the sun warming his back thinking about the unfairness of her burden.

"I was so proud of you yesterday, Lil. You were so beautiful sitting at the table selling the books. I could tell the women admired you."

She laughed, "For putting up with you?"

He laughed and said, "You make me happy!"

She walked across the room, kissed him on the mouth and declared, "I'm happy!"

He took a sip of coffee and thought about the members of yesterday's group. He was reminded of another group of citizens, equally sincere, equally committed to their duty within the community: the good people of the local Selective Service, the Draft Board.

Dan compared the two groups of people - each in their own way representing the community: his community. They were different but, in many ways, they seemed the same. Then, so long ago, the Draft Board had sent him into exile. Now, the readers group had welcomed him home.

Like Odysseus, he was finally home. Lilly brought his coffee and he hugged her around the waist, pulling her to him and holding her tight.

She ran her fingers through his hair, "How about a haircut?"

# Author's Notes

It was many years ago when I began writing about my time in the village of Hoa An and the teachers and dear friends I met there who would influence my life forever. By their daily kindness and humble wisdom, they had opened the door to Asia for me. All I had to do was pay attention.

It is sometimes said that writers are motivated by a need to understand, or at least wrestle with, some of life's mysteries. In *Auspicious Journey* I was driven to understand *Why?* Why had there been this war and what was my part in it?

If I believe in a world of cause and effect, as opposed to random chaos, then I must believe there has to be some larger reason for this, or any, war. Because of the great suffering of the old ones, the women, and the children, and all the men and women at war, who died then and are still dying, that reason, the real cause, the *Why*, must somehow carry equal weight in the sands of time.

However, as the date of publication for *Auspicious Journey* drew nearer I realized I still hadn't discovered *Why*. Eventually however, three main constructs began to emerge.

The first theme was that the war in Viet Nam sprung from the unrelenting national and personal angst of being a slave-holding nation. Held hostage by our steadfast denial, the horrible, crippling effects of the realities of slavery have been passed from generation to the next without even an attempt at resolution. From "Gook" to "Sand Nigger," Iraq was just more of the same.

The second theme was the constant, unquestioned inevitability of the victimization of the Vietnamese women who were brutalized by rape, prostitution and snuff crimes, all behaviors consistent with the institutional treatment of women as a convenient underclass.

The third theme was that these events have exposed the fragility of the belief of white/male superiority we hold so dear.

Are we really waging war after war to protect such unsustainable nonsense?

When do we begin to understand that emotional intimacy, love if you will, can never be taken by force or influence or entitlement? When do we begin to understand that *love can only be given* and that the power of that gift is greater than the power of any army, or any amount of wealth, or influence.

And when do we begin to understand that love, that greatest of gifts, can only really be shared between equals? Thus, from Jesus to Jefferson, its promise beats in the heart of every child, every woman, every man.

I thought about that one day in Hoa An when the elders had requested that I meet with them where the trails intersected by the graveyard. Because of my habits of Western thought, and because I had worked with the priests at the Buddhist school, I asked to meet their priests.

They explained they had no priests. I was intrigued, but not convinced. I repeated my request and they again replied that they had no priests.

So, I asked, "What is your religion?"

One of the elders stepped forward, bowed, and said, "Luong."

Luong? I had never heard of it. I couldn't find it anywhere and I looked everywhere.

When I returned to Viet Nam in 2005, I purchased a copy of *When Heaven and Earth Changed Places* from a street vendor in Ho Chi Minh City. Written by Le Ly Hayslip, I became aware of her association with the East-West foundation in Oakland, California, and attempted without success to contact her there. By 2018, *Auspicious Journey* had been published and my presence on the internet allowed them to feel comfortable enough to go ahead and provide me with her email address.

Sometime later we were talking on the phone when she used the word "luong" in conversation.

I was so excited! I yelled, "Luong! Luong! What does it mean? What does it mean?"

She chuckled and explained, "When the French came to Viet Nam they were determined to convert everyone to Catholicism. They lined all the people up and asked them what their religion was. Wishing to be polite, the people bowed their heads and said, "Luong."

I persisted, "What does it mean? What does it mean?"

She chuckled again and said, "It means I have no religion - everything is sacred."

And there it was - everything I had been looking for in one self explanatory statement, the simple truth I had been searching for from the first it time I heard it where the trails crossed by the graveyard, so many years ago.

*I have no religion - everything is sacred.*

# Acknowledgments and Gratitudes

Writers are often seen as solitary creatures wrestling with the passion of their latest work into print while still in their pajamas. While some of this may be true, in my case, I am pretty certain that, this book, or any other, would never be written, or certainly not published, without the support, kindness, and generosity, of those listed below.

A very special gratitude to Samantha Camblin whose determination and unique editing skills rescued the manuscript to Summer of Love from permanent residence in the trash bin.

A special gratitude to Sophia Crescioli for her gracious permission to use her especially unique and evocative photograph for the cover.

Los Osos Writer's Group: Anne R. Allen, Christine Ahern, Laurie Brallier, Chester Perryess, and Sidonie Weidenkeller, for their patience, and understanding.

Sister, reader, and "first fan" Faye Reimel.

Valued Readers: Sally Ann Thornberry, Karen Hardman, Jim West.

Clean copy editor and best brother: Jess West

Consultants, supporters and friends: Jeff Stein, Richard Madeira, Robert Dyer, Salvador Ruiz, Terry Zolezzi, Leonard Manzella, David Congalton, Bill Chapman, Frank Bernal, David Black, Bob Wood, David McNamara.

Anne and Alex Gough, for constant and untiring support.

To Julie and the rest of the staff at the Country Touch Cafe.

And most importantly, that good-hearted publisher Peter Werrenrath.